WHAT'S FOR DINNER?

JAMES SCHUYLER

BLACK SPARROW PRESS : SANTA BARBARA : 1978

WHAT'S FOR DINNER? Copyright © 1978 by James Schuyler.

All rights reserved. Printed in the United States of America. No part of this book may be used or reproduced in any manner whatsoever without written permission except in the case of brief quotations embodied in critical articles and reviews. For information address Black Sparrow Press, P.O. Box 3993, Santa Barbara, CA 93105.

The cover drawing is by Jane Freilicher.

LIBRARY OF CONGRESS CATALOGING IN PUBLICATION DATA
Schuyler, James.
     What's for dinner?

     1. Title.
PZ4.S396Wh   [PS3569.C56]   813'.5'4   78-16914
ISBN 0-87685-382-3
ISBN 0-87685-383-1 signed cloth
ISBN 0-87685-381-5 pbk.

for Anne Dunn

What's For Dinner?

Chapter I

It was a lovely light living room. Or it would have been, had not a previous owner found quick-growing conifer seedlings an irresistible bargain. When the sun set, a few red beams would struggle in, disclosing in their passage the dust of which the air at times seems largely composed. Mary C. Taylor—the laughing Charlotte of the class of 19**—found the sweet mood brought on by contemplation of the spick-and-spanness in which her husband Norris perused and, presumably, memorized the evening paper, soured.

"It seems to me all I do is dust this room." She put on the bridge lamp at her elbow, in hopes of fighting light with light.

"It isn't dust, it's pollen." Norris was never so absorbed as not to leave a trickle of attention running.

"Not when it gets in here," she said tranquilly, as she followed the course of a large and furtive basset towards an easy chair. "Deirdre wants her dribble cloth."

Norris, deep in the mendacities of one of the columnists who shaped his thought, made no comment.

"I said, would you give her her cloth."

(9)

"Why should I?"

"Because it's under your elbow." Lottie, as some called her, crossed the room—no easy task, for it was amply furnished as the yard—lifted his arm and abstracted a square of oil cloth, then lifted the dog's head and spread it over the chair arm. The dog sighed and returned to its basket in the kitchen.

"I wonder what you'll do when I'm gone? Are you planning to remarry?"

"What's for dinner?"

"I suppose you'll go on some sort of trip and meet somebody so it's no good trying to figure out who you'll pick. Meat loaf."

"Perhaps I intend to predecease you." His wife left the room. She returned, carrying a perfume atomizer. Placing herself at an angle to a sunbeam, she rapidly squeezed the bulb.

"It's only water. To see if it will lay the dust."

"And does it?"

"I can't tell. I think so. Or it may just stir it up. Or it's other dust that rushes in to take its place."

"A lawn sprinkler might be more to your purpose."

Mrs Taylor shrugged and put the atomizer on the mantle. Her husband frowned.

"You see," she said contentedly. "You wouldn't like it a bit if I didn't keep this room scrupulously tidy. Not that I expect ever to reach the exalted standard set by your mother."

"I suppose she has given up dusting, now that she herself is dust." He spoke with the certitude of an accredited agnostic. "Did you say meat loaf? I surmise you're kidding."

Deirdre, her dugs grazing the carpet pile, slunk back. Once more she was foiled in an attempt to make off with her dribble cloth and destroy it.

"Red sky at night—is it sailors or shepherds who are so delighted by that?" Before Norris could answer, if that was his plan, the sun set, the dust vanished, and the doorbell sounded in the pattern of "Shave and a haircut, two bits."

"It's the Delehanteys."

Norris leaned backwards with a lipless grin.

(10)

"I'm sure I told you; in fact, you know I did. For pity's sake let's put on some lights," she said as she did so, "or I don't know what they'll think." A painting of an Indian encampment sprang into view.

Norris went and, to the toppling of a Benares tray, admitted their guests, who were six: Mr and Mrs Bryan Delehantey, old Mrs Delehantey, Patrick and Michael, the twins, and a cat on a leash.

They made short work of shedding their wraps, and were soon milling about the living room. "It is a beauteous evening," the elder Mrs Delehantey claimed, "calm and free," as she achieved her goal, a straight back chair all wooden knobs and spirals. Perched above its taloned feet, Biddy reminded herself of something she had read about a Chinese empress who looked like a wise old monkey. Her daughter-in-law's Scandanavian interiors gave small scope for such a view.

"Calm and freezing is more like it," said the younger, and larger, Mrs Delehantey (Maureen). As usual, her robust frame appeared freshly back from the upholsterer. "Why it's Mary Lottie!" she .exclaimed, as though surprised at finding same in her own living room, a room which seemed all thrust and menace to the speaker. She gazed about her with a large smile. "Oh! the plants, the plants." She studied some evacuees from the jungle floor who found the lighting altogether to their taste.

"We don't know where to sit," one of the twins said in a foggy bass.

"Sit anywhere boys," Biddy said, "so long as you don't sit on your old Gran."

"And see you sit up straight," their mother said.

"And keep your mouths shut," their father said.

"And mind Twing," their mother said. The boys subsided on a bench in a misleading state of catatonia. "Pussy pines so if we leave her alone: we knew you wouldn't mind if we brought her." Silence was the most the Taylors could muster in reply.

When they saw in what the appetite-whetters were served, the conversation turned naturally to the subject of collecting. Spoons, salt and peppers, towels stolen from distant athletic clubs with matching ash tray: then Biddy put in her two cents worth.

"Do you know what I collect, boys? Happiness, that's what I

collect."

Maureen moved uneasily. "I think Twing wants to see her friend Deirdre." The cat in question was lying on her back, idly ripping at some ball fringe.

"America, the melting pot," Norris said. "Let's hope their union will not be blessed with issue."

"I'll take her," Michael hastily offered.

"You stay where you are," said his father, a Solomon of the suburbs. "Patrick can do it." Sluggishly, the youth led the reluctant cat from the room and, under cover of yowl and howl, subjected the contents of the refrigerator to a swift and circumspect diminishment.

"She doesn't want to see her," Patrick said on their return.

"I gathered," Norris said.

"The days grow shorter," Biddy said.

"I don't think so, Mother," Bryan said in a loud voice. He sometimes had difficulty in hearing what she said—she often spoke with food in her mouth—and deduced that her hearing was failing. "This is February."

"Today," Norris said, "is the first of March."

"Isn't this leap year?" his wife asked.

"I seriously doubt it."

"What I mean," Biddy said, "is that at my age the days, though I sleep less and they are therefore longer, seem much shorter and to go by more quickly. More rapidly, in fact, than I can say. It is a paradox." Mrs Taylor shivered.

"You'll live a long time yet, Mother," her daughter-in-law said in a voice as bright as a scoured sink. Biddy looked inscrutable.

"Please pass the edible oddments," Norris said.

"Well boys, don't just sit there," their father barked. "Not you Patrick, Michael can do it. And remember not to offer yourself any."

"Perhaps Patrick would be so kind as to help Twing down off of the mantle," Lottie said. "Those figurines . . ."

Bryan laughed heartily. "Haven't you heard the expression, Sure footed as a cat? Especially true of Siamese." Twing curled up behind the Seth Thomas clock, slightly dislodging it from its alignment.

"Ever hear the one about the dog who howled in the night?" Norris asked.

Lottie opened her mouth to speak, closed it, then said, "I think I'll just go look in the oven." The gaze with which her husband followed her exit from the room was one of amusement not unmixed with pity.

In the kitchen Lottie opened the oven and rattled the roaster without bothering to open it. The she went to a cupboard, took a bottle of vodka and had a swig. She went to the sink and turned on a tap, apparently intending to top up the bottle. Instead she shrugged, drank again, recorked the spirits and put it back. "A little nip never hurt anyone," she said half-aloud.

"Well," Bryan was saying on her return, "Hasn't either of you anything to contribute to the conversation?"

Patrick cleared his throat, coughed, and rumbled, "How old is Deirdre?"

"Nine," Norris said.

"Eleven," his wife said. "I know, because we got her the year of my appendectomy."

"My stars," Maureen said. "Is that eleven years ago? I remember so well going to see you in the hospital and when I got home the twins were sickening with scarletina. I was so afraid I might have given it to you, in your weakened condition."

"Yes. I confess I was a little alarmed myself, but I'm afraid hypochondria runs in my family. And in Norris's too. You brought me a perfectly lovely azalea which we later planted out. But you wouldn't know it now—it's grown to be quite a bush."

"What color is it?" Michael asked.

"Salmon."

"You needn't talk as though you took any interest in gardening," Bryan said. "Just getting these lummoxes to tend the lawn takes my next to last breath."

"We could do with a healthy lummox," Norris said. "All our yard man likes to do is hoe. I think because he likes to lean on it."

"We're going to have more snow yet this year," Biddy said. "I can tell by my joints." She exhibited her swollen knuckles.

"How painful," Lottie said. "I often wonder if I'm not developing bursitis. In the mornings I can hardly bend my left elbow. Some days."

"That's because you sleep on your left side," Norris explained.

"At least I don't sleep on my back. We all know what that leads to."

"Snoring," Maureen said.

Patrick guffawed and his father glared at the twins. Michael, who had been chafing his thighs, turned beet red.

"I think," Lottie said, rising to her feet, "I can begin putting things on the table."

"I'll come with you," Norris said.

"Don't bother." Nevertheless, he followed her from the room.

"No cocktails," Biddy said knowingly.

"I thought that might be the case," Bryan said. "And took the necessary precaution before we left."

"So did I," Maureen said, "and I intend to go right on matching you drink for drink, so you needn't give me one of your looks."

Biddy, who had never touched a drop in her Presbyterian life said, "I consider this most unsuitable in front of the lads." Said lads were wearing their deaf and dumb look. "I don't know where you got the habit: your father was a complete abstainer," she said to her gigantic son.

"I've sometimes wondered about that," Bryan said in a teasing tone.

"The clock!" Maureen exclained under her breath and quickly crossed the room; or as quickly as some sidetables would allow. Twing, shifting to a more comfortable position, had pushed the clock to the edge of the mantle. "Here," Maureen said, passing the cat to the boys, "see she keeps out of mischief." Twing began kneading bread in Michael's lap, who said "Ow!" in a loud tone.

"Stop bellowing over nothing," Bryan said. "If you think a cat scratch is the worst that's going to happen to you . . ."

"Oh lay off for a while," Maureen said.

"I'm sure the boys try," Biddy said. "They're the apples of my eyes. I well remember that when I was their age nothing I did could

(14)

seen to please my grandmother, God rest her soul. I was always tripping over my own feet, just like the boys. 'Don't sit down like a spoonful of mush,' she used to say to me. I can hear her now."

"Which grandmother was that?" Michael asked.

"Your great-grandmother Bellowes. She had a light hand with pastry but a strong one with the switch."

"You make good pies," Patrick said.

"Look at them," Bryan said, whom the twins closely resembled, not least in bulk, "food, food, food."

"I said," Maureen said, "that's enough. I can never imagine how Mary Lottie keeps this room so spit tidy: there's not a thing in it that isn't a dust-catcher. And without a maid."

"Oh," Biddy said. "I thought she had Mrs Gompers come in once a week to help out."

"She'd never let her in *here*," Maureen said. "Mrs Gompers is just for heavy work: waxing the kitchen floor and so on. She'd reduce those—" she pointed to a laden knick-knack stand, "to smithereens. I ought to know. I'll never forget the day she dropped that stack of Spode plates. I rushed into the pantry and she was standing there shaking her head and saying, 'Butterfingers.' I let her finish out the day, but that was the end of that."

"With your vim," Biddy said, "you don't really need the help. Not that it mightn't be a nice change for you to get out more."

"Oh, I'm not complaining," Maureen said.

In the kitchen Lottie was saying, "I think we should have offered cocktails."

"Bryan already had a few," Norris said. "Couldn't you smell it?"

"So had Maureen. Bourbon smells even worse than it tastes." She was lifting a turkey onto a platter while he funneled California claret from a jug into a decanter. "Could you reach down that sauce boat?" Norris opened the cupboard and remarked in an idle tone, "I see somebody else has had a few."

His wife didn't answer, but her cheeks were red, and not from the oven.

At the table Norris said, "I expect you boys would like the drumsticks."

"They take what's served them," Bryan said.

"Aren't they old enough for half a glass of wine?" Lottie asked. "They look it."

"Oh sure," Bryan said. "I'd rather have them drink in front of me than behind my back."

"As you did behind your father's?" Biddy said with a twinkle. "Remember the time he smelled beer on your breath? My, he certainly gave you a hiding."

"And I was none the worse for it," Bryan said, surveying his sons. "May I refill your glass, Lottie?"

"Why, yes, thank you." She was toying with the food on her plate rather than eating.

"Fellow told me an interesting story today," Bryan said, "at the office. Man I've worked with twenty years. Actually, it wasn't at the office: it was at lunch—Mariano's (glad you're not having ravioli tonight). Seems he has this son going on for nineteen maybe, in his second year in college. Or they *thought* he was in college. Letters kept coming pretty regularly, asking for money of course—some extra expense, lab fees, or like that. Well as luck would have it, business took Hal into the area of the college so he thought he'd drop in, surprise the kid. And you know what? He wasn't there. Vanished into thin air. Luckily, Hal knew his son's roommate from the year before—knew his name anyway—and he was there all right. As soon as Hal introduced himself the kid broke down and admitted he'd been forwarding Hal Junior's letters: young Hal hadn't even registered for the fall term but was living in New York—Greenwich Village or some place like that, living with some girl and off of the money he was supposed to use for college. Hal was so disgusted he wanted to drop the matter right there but his wife went all to pieces and insisted. So—can you believe it?—they're paying him an allowance until he gets on his feet and decides if he wants to go on with college. I would have shown him the sole of my boot."

"He should have confided in his mother," Maureen said.

"Was he always a wild boy?" Lottie asked. "Do they think he was using drugs?"

"My sympathies are with the family of the girl," Biddy said. "Just imagine how they must feel. Why they may not even know where she is! I don't understand all this running away. And the places they run to sound so simply dreadful."

"Sowing wild oats is not exactly a novelty," Norris said. "One of my uncles passed some bum checks in college—forged his father's signature. The old man popped him into a clinic for a year and he grew up to be excessively scrupulous about money. Always paid cash. For everything: wouldn't even have a mortgage on his house."

"That," Bryan said, "is financially foolish. But I must say, I think a little less of Hal. Weak-kneed, I call it."

Lottie held out her glass and Bryan filled it.

"Oh judge not lest," Biddy said. "You never know all the ins and outs of family life. There may be extenuating circumstances. Who knows? It may bring them all the closer together in the end. So often a troubled passage is the prelude to peaceful seas."

"And a prosperous voyage," Norris said.

Lottie belched quietly. "That uncle of yours—the forger—was he a clergyman's son?"

"Yes, he was, and please don't tell me clergymen's children always turn out badly."

"They often do," Lottie insisted. "People expect them to be models of goodness knows what and they rebel."

"May I offer you a little more of the breast, Mrs Delehantey?" Norris asked.

"Oh no thank you," Biddy said. "Well, just a morsel."

"No seconds for the boys," Bryan said. "They're supposed to be in training."

"What are you in training for?" Norris asked.

"Well, one of you answer," Bryan said.

"I was waiting for my mouth to be empty," Patrick said. "Spring training for the football squad."

"We go out for football," Michael explained.

"You've got the builds for it," Norris said. "Though I don't remember seeing you at any of the home games last fall."

"We weren't old enough then," Michael said.

"You only went to one," Lottie said, twirling the stem of her glass,

(17)

which was again empty. Bryan didn't offer to fill it, so she did so herself.

"I don't know where they find the time," Maureen said. "Both my boys are in the school orchestra—Patrick plays the oboe while Michael studies trumpet. You must come to the Easter concert. I'm sure it will be lovely. Mr Marks is a most dedicated teacher."

Under the table Patrick nudged his brother at this allusion to 'Fruity' Marks. Happily married, father of three, Mr Marks had a habit of resting his hand on a boy's shoulder while reviewing a score.

"At the seminary I attended," Biddy said, "we had an all string orchestra. I played second violin." She put her head on one side, held up her hands and made sawing motions. "Can you picture it?"

"Why I never knew that, Biddy," Maureen said.

"Don't get me started on the days at old Sem! I implore you. There's simply no end to what I remember. There was one girl— Lucy something: now what was her last name? I know it as well as I know my own. Oh, it's right on the tip of my tongue. It's something like Jones or Smith only not quite that common. Miller. Lucy Miller. We used to call her 'cat's cradle', because of the eerie screeching noise she produced from her instrument. And the odd thing was that no one worked harder at her practicing than Lucy 'cat's cradle' Miller. At recitals she was quietly asked to go through the motions without actually playing."

Lottie laughed rather loudly at this story.

"More stuffing, anyone?" Norris asked.

"At my school," Maureen said, "there was a girl we called Kitty, but that was because she had such a catty tongue."

"Lucy Miller," Biddy said, "later married most advantageously and moved west. I wonder what's become of her, if she's still alive."

Norris asked to have the wine passed, poured himself half a glass, and set the decanter down by his place.

"Perhaps someone else would like some," his wife said.

"Perhaps a smidgen," Maureen said.

"Dad?" Patrick said.

"No," Bryan said, "definitely not."

"Let me help you clear," Maureen offered, rising to her feet and suiting action to her words.

"We'll just dump them in the pantry," Lottie said. The dessert course followed: an ice box pie with a graham cracker crust.

"I know you don't take coffee, Biddy, so let me make you a nice pot of tea."

"I wouldn't dream of it—a whole pot just for me! But if you have any tea bags . . ."

"And I," Lottie said, "wouldn't dream of that. It's no trouble." In the kitchen she rested her hands on the sink and sighed. She opened the cupboard, looked at the bottle of vodka, then firmly closed the door. She felt dizzy. All the same, she soon returned with tea in a small ornate Victorian pot. "I hope you like English Breakfast mix. It's the only kind Norris will tolerate."

"What a lovely thing that is," Biddy said, regarding the pot. "An heirloom piece, I don't doubt. It seems to me Grandmother Fowler had one not unlike it—a set. I wonder what ever became of all those things? She had twelve children and one of my aunts was what you could only call rather grasping. At the time she passed on—Grandmother Fowler, not my aunt—we were living in rather a small and crowded house and just hadn't the room for some of the things that might have come to us."

"My wife and I," Norris said, "were both rich in childless aunts and uncles. So it all winds up here."

"And what will become of it when we're gone? Sometimes I'm tempted to have a white elephant sale. What am I bid for this sideboard?"

"Things have their associations," Norris said.

"You must let me help with the dishes," Maureen said.

"Heavens, no. I wouldn't know what to do with myself if there weren't a few dishes to wash up now and then. Shall we go into the living room? Bring your coffee—and your tea, Biddy."

"One cup is all I can manage these days," Biddy said. "That's why it's such a shame to make a whole pot, just for me."

"You could pour it off, for iced tea," Maureen said. "Though I guess it's scarcely the time of year."

Lottie led the march between the china cupboards to the living

(19)

room, the boys politely bringing up the rear.

"Piss on you," Patrick muttered.

"Shove it up your bung," his brother replied.

"Spring, spring: will it never come?" Maureen asked when she had regained the overstuffed chair she had earlier vacated.

"There was that time in the eighteenth century," Norris said, "I believe it was, when summer never came. The black summer."

Maureen seemed stunned. "I can't picture it. Whatever did they do? Didn't people starve?"

"I believe many did. There was a general panic, of course."

"I can remember a summer almost as bad as that," Biddy said. "The corn went all mouldy in the ear. I was too young to remember much about it—just the general consternation. And my father taking me out to see what had happened to the corn. It made me cry."

"Anyone mind if I smoke this?" Bryan asked, waving back and forth a large cigar.

There were few things Lottie hated more ("It gets in the curtains," was her usual morning after complaint, "and stays for days"). "I'll fetch you an ashtray. I think of your after dinner cigar as a kind of tradition, Bryan."

"You given up on the weed, Norris?" Bryan asked.

"Three years ago, as a matter of fact." They had had this conversation before. "When my doctor heard me cough, and I told him how many packs I smoked, he said, 'You better make a choice, and you better make it fast.' So I did. The first month was unadulterated hell, I don't mind saying, and I gained ten pounds. Very rough on Mary Charlotte."

"There was no living with him," his wife said as she placed an enormous cloisonné bowl at Bryan's elbow. "Still, like most things, it passed."

Patrick yawned widely. "Close your mouth," his father said, "and keep it shut."

"Where's Twing?" Maureen asked in sudden alarm.

"She's here," Patrick said. The cat was asleep beside him on the bench. Deirdre wandered into the room, sniffed loudly at the cat and began to lick its ear.

"And the lion shall lie down with the lamb," Biddy said. "One of my aunts had a canary that she let fly loose, and that bird would drink out of the same bowl as their cat. The cat had been altered."

"I wasn't aware," Norris said, "that that changed their attitude toward their natural prey."

"As sure as I'm sitting here," Biddy twisted about in her chair, "that cat never laid a paw on that canary."

"Oh, I wasn't doubting your veracity: it was the explanation that surprised me. Perhaps it had an unusually passive nature. There are these exceptions."

"That cat was as great a mouser as you could hope to meet in a long summer's day. My aunt used to get quite cross, because I took the side of the mice and wanted to make him let them go. I was very young and understood nothing about germs."

Lottie stifled a yawn. "Excuse me," she said, and went out to the kitchen. Norris got up and silently followed her. They returned shortly. Lottie stumbled slightly on the edge of a carpet. The others took no notice.

"We really ought to be running along," Maureen said.

"Oh no," Lottie said. "Bryan hasn't begun to finish his cigar."

"Yes," Norris said, "what's all the rush?"

"It's partly the boys," Maureen said. "What with school and training and their music they seem to need a great deal of sleep."

"Slug-a-beds," Bryan said. "They can't sit down to study without falling asleep over their notebooks."

"I ran two miles before breakfast," Patrick protested.

"Yes, it's Michael who's in love with his pillow," their mother said fondly. "Sometimes I still have to pull the covers right off him."

"You ought to give the job of rousting them out to me," Bryan said, carefully knocking the ash off his cigar. "This seems too fine an object to be used as an ashtray."

Lottie shrugged. "That's what my great uncle used it for, and I certainly haven't any other use for it. I'll leave it to you in my will." This was greeted by some rather hollow chuckles.

"I hope we're not keeping you from any of your favorite TV programs," Biddy said.

(21)

"We hardly turn the thing on," Norris said, "except for the news, and the odd special event. Like the President's speech."

"Oh, did you catch that too?" Maureen said. "I thought he made some telling points." Norris let this pass, as the two families voted different tickets.

"Yes," Biddy said, "the novelty wears off. Why I remember when we had a crystal set with earphones, and how the children used to wrangle over who was going to listen. Personally, it would be all the same to me if TV had never been invented."

"Oh Biddy," Maureen said, "you know you wouldn't miss your serials for the world."

"I hardly know one from the other. But I feel the need of a little rest in the afternoon and since I don't nap, I like something to occupy my attention. Some of the acting is very well done."

Maureen laughed. "The other afternoon I heard the most hair raising screams coming from the set, so I went in to see what it was all about. This man was threatening to choke a woman with a necktie and there was Mother Delehantey sound asleep in her chair, literally dead to the world. The moment I turned down the volume, she woke up."

"Dead to the world," Biddy said. "I shan't be sorry to go when my time comes. In fact, I would much rather go than become bedridden and dependent."

"That's enough of that," Bryan said. "You're a good deal sprier than I am, young woman."

"I imagine we'll all be around a while longer," Norris said. "May I offer anyone a highball?" Demurrers were general.

"What's in a highball?" Patrick asked.

"Nothing you're going to have," Bryan said.

"Whiskey and soda. Or, whiskey and water. In a tall glass," Norris explained.

"Why is it called a highball?" Michael asked, not to be outdone by his brother.

"The high part is easy," Norris said, "but I can't say how the ball got in there."

"A lot of things have names there isn't any reason for," Biddy said.

"No one could ever tell me why a surrey was called that. Though I can't imagine why I wanted to know. 'The Surrey With the Fringe on Top.' Now that's a catchy tune."

"All the tunes are catchy in *Oklahoma*. Maureen and I saw it when it was running in New York. And the movie, too, of course."

"That wasn't yesterday," Maureen said. "Which reminds me, Mary Lottie, I was talking on the phone to Mag yesterday. It's wonderful to me how she does for herself, alone in that big old house. I came right out and said to her—not yesterday, another time—why didn't she sell the house and move into an apartment? In an apartment, I thought she'd feel the loneliness less, after her husband's demise."

"It was so sudden," Lottie said.

"Yes, wasn't it. But she says there she knows where she can lay her hand right on anything she wants. She hasn't a fear in the world of housebreakers. I didn't like to come out and say it, but what concerned me more was the thought of her having some kind of accident, and all alone there. Like slipping and falling in the tub."

"Which might also happen in an apartment," Norris said.

"Oh, with Mag's personality she'd soon be on terms with all her neighbors. They'd notice if she wasn't about."

"Or she could lie in the tub and scream," Norris said. "That would fetch them."

"A serious fall is no joking matter," Maureen said, "not at Mag's age. But you always like to look on the lighter side, don't you, Norris."

"I don't believe in anticipating trouble. If I started counting up all the things that might happen right in his house I'd never get out of this chair again. Read in the paper about a woman who was electrocuted when a hair drier fell in the tub."

"For goodness sake," Lottie said, "let's get away from tubs."

"Yes indeed let's," Biddy said. "They're treacherous things."

Deirdre left the room and returned with a large rubber bone in her jaws. "Why Deirdre Taylor," Lottie said, "you know that's not allowed in here." Like a tugboat, the dog slowly turned and waddled out of the room.

"Isn't it wonderful, the way they understand," Biddy said.

Twing now decided to make a circuit of the room, giving its unpleasant Siamese cry. "They love to talk," Biddy observed. Twing finally elected for Bryan and leapt up. In doing so, both cat and Bryan's lap became covered with cigar ash.

"Oh gosh," Bryan said, "look what you've done, kitty."

"Brush it on the rug," Lottie said. "Ashes are supposed to be good for the nap. Like damp tea leaves—not that I ever use them."

"Damp tea leaves!" Biddy exclaimed. "I haven't thought of those in years. They used to give the carpet a certain smell, funny but nice. I wonder why customs like that go out of style? It worked very well."

"Perhaps the perfecting of the vacuum cleaner had something to do with it," Norris said.

Finally the Delehantey's took their departure, though not before a scramble with Twing over her leash. When the last goodbye and the protestations of pleasure and the praise of the food had all been said, and the driveway light turned off and the front door locked and chained, Lottie more or less flopped into a chair. "I don't know that I think Mag's personality is anything so out of the way," she said.

"She's a cheery little soul," Norris said.

"Sometimes it grates. All that cooing. It isn't so much that you wonder what she's really thinking as I wonder if she's thinking anything at all." She got to her feet. "I'm not going to touch a dish tonight, but I do have to straighten up the kitchen a little. You go up to bed."

"Yes," Norris said. "I'll do that." He was not yet asleep when he heard his wife stumble on the stair on her own way up.

At the Delehantey's the evening received short review: as a family, they were one and all devoted to sleep and plenty of it.

"I wonder what gives a person the idea you can't smell vodka," Bryan asked as he shed his garments. "Did you catch her breath?"

"Secret tippling," Maureen said. "It never ends well. It went to my heart when she almost fell over that rug. I must say, Norris puts a good face on it."

"Norris isn't a lawyer for nothing."

There came a light tapping. It was Biddy. "Twing was scratching at my door." She was holding the purring cat in her arms.

"Give her to me, Mother," Maureen said. "The lock on the kitchen door doesn't always catch. Come with me, Twingy-poo."

In the twins' room the light was already off. After a time, Patrick began to breathe heavily. Shortly, and with practiced stealth, Michael got out of his bed and into his brother's. They jerked each other off, Patrick never ceasing to feign the breathing sounds of sleep. A box of Kleenex stood convenient on the night table between their beds.

Chapter II

1

"If your wife seems a little euphoric," the nurse said, "you must realize that she is taking paraldehyde, which tends to induce a state of—uh, euphoria."

"I know," Norris said. "The doctor told me."

"She's waiting for you in the sun room." The nurse pointed down the corridor, where various patients were sitting or ambling about. It was indeed a sunny room, the curtains and furniture done in a cheerful leafy chintz. Lottie was seated at a table with two other women and a man playing bridge. They were between hands, and when she saw her husband she rose to her feet with a radiant smile.

"Why Norris! How nice."

"Weren't you expecting me?"

"Of course I was expecting you, but that doesn't make it any less nice to see you, or of you to come see me."

Norris kissed her on the cheek. "But I'm interrupting your game."

"Oh tush. Mrs Brice will take my hand. Oh Mrs Brice, wouldn't you like to sit in for me while I visit with my boy friend?"

Mrs Brice was a heavy woman in purple knit. She was sitting with her hands in her lap and her ankles crossed, doing nothing. "I'll just spoil it for the others. I'm not any good."

"It's just a pastime," Lottie said. "We none of us are exactly Olympic bridge champs."

"You'll be my partner," the man of the foursome said. "If you get the bid, I'll be dummy and can help you play the hand. You'll see. It will all go swimmingly."

Mrs Brice got up and joined them in a way that showed she felt she had no choice in the matter. "Clubs, diamonds, hearts, spades," she said. "That's how it goes, isn't it?"

"I'll write down the Goren point count system for you," the man said. "Then you can refer to it when you count up your hand."

"I'm sure it's not going to be much fun for any of you," Mrs Brice said.

"Think of it as a bridge lesson," Lottie said. "That's what we're all here for: to learn something. Bridge isn't anything so important but you'll enjoy it. You'll enjoy mastering something new. That's what I say: we're all here to learn."

"That's not why I'm here," one of the women said. "I'm here because my husband hates me. Is it my deal?"

Lottie led Norris away. "Come see my room. I'm so lucky to have fallen heir to one of the single rooms, even if it is small. Two of the rooms even have four beds in them—I wouldn't really care for that. Though of course I could cope with it, if destiny willed. I bless my stars that my own affliction is a relatively easy one to deal with. Take Mrs Brice. If we let her, she'd just sit, sit, sit all day and all evening—except for meals, of course. And she doesn't even know she's in a depression. Her only son and his family, I happen to know. But she never alludes to it: it's all bottled up inside her."

"How's the food?" Norris asked.

"Too starchy, but on the whole, not bad. I mean it is hospital fare." She put her hands on her hips and smoothed down her dress. "I'm certainly going to have to diet when I get out of here."

"You look fine," Norris said. "In fact, you look a good deal better than when you came in. I think you were underweight."

"Probably. It's often the case with people who have my problem."

"So this is your little hidey-hole," Norris said. The room was indeed small and narrow, and, like the sun room, dominated by a chintz—in this case, one with a pattern of ivy and oriental poppies. The walls were painted a milky shade of lime.

"The first night I was here I thought those poppies were out to get me," Lottie giggled. "Fortunately, the doctor had ordered something to make me sleep. But I've gotten used to it—even rather to like it. I suppose because it's *my* room. You sit in the chair. I'll perch here on the bed."

"I see you've received a lot of floral tributes." Norris regarded her deep window sill, crammed with potted plants. A bouquet of gladiolas in mixed colors towered on the desk.

"Guess who sent me the glads? You'll never: Mag Carpenter. Wasn't it thoughtful? Isn't it kind? And so just like her. But let's not talk about me. Tell me about you: how's the office?"

"All is in the capable hands of Miss Finch. But I'll bet it's not the office you're wondering about: it's the house."

"Frankly, I haven't got a worry in the world. I suppose it's this stuff I take. My partner over-trumped me earlier and it seemed to me like the funniest thing I'd ever come up against. I really had to hold myself in to keep from going on a laughing jag."

A nurse with a trolley appeared in the door and rapped on the frame. "Medication time," she said.

"Heavens: is it four o'clock already?" Lottie hopped off the bed and accepted a small plastic cup from which she drank. The nurse made a face.

"I don't know how you can stomach it, Mrs Taylor," she said. "The smell alone . . ."

"The funny thing about it," Lottie said, "I'm afraid is that I've almost gotten to like it. I try not to breathe in people's faces, but yesterday one of the patients turned quite pale and said, 'Embalming fluid! I smell embalming fluid!' I explained that paraldehyde and formaldehyde smell alike, because they're related. I'm afraid she thought for a while there that she was hallucinating."

"I must push on," the nurse said, continuing on her errand of mercy.

A look of almost worry passed over Lottie's face. "The doctor says it won't all be roses when they change my medication. It frightens me: suppose I plunge back into feeling the way I did?"

"It's a transition," Norris said, "back to your normal self. One step at a time."

"That's what the head nurse keeps saying. I don't feel blue so I won't be blue. How is Mrs Gompers working out?"

"Hasn't broken anything so far, to the best of my knowledge. Of course I made it plain which cupboards are strictly out of bounds. And I carried some of the things from the living room up to the attic: why tempt fate?"

"It makes me feel funny," Lottie said, "thinking of people like Mrs Gompers knowing all about me. It makes me feel horrid."

"Sympathy . . ." Norris began.

"And I don't want sympathy. When I get out of here what I'm going to want is a drink. A fat lot of good sympathy is going to do me then."

"You underestimate your own will power. When you come home, and realize what strides you've taken, you won't want a drink."

"Oh I don't want to be an alcoholic—a common drunk, that's for sure. But how can anyone know how he or she will stand up to temptation? It's so easy to think, 'One little nip won't hurt.' Then it's the primrose path to hell all over again. There's a woman in here now who . . ."

A young woman with heavy eyebrows, a blank expression and wearing a flowered wrapper came and stood in the door. "Is that your husband?" she said.

"Why, yes, it is," Lottie said in her new bright voice. "This is Norris, Bertha. I'm sorry, but I've forgotten your last name."

"So have I," Bertha said.

"Oh now, I'm sure you can remember it if you try. You knew it yesterday."

"That's not my fault. A lot of people think I look like Elizabeth

Taylor. Do you?"

"Do you mean Elizabeth Taylor, the famous actress?" Norris hedged.

"Yes, that one."

Norris decided to go whole hog. "As a matter of fact, I do see quite a resemblance. I imagine your smile is like hers."

Bertha frowned. "Some people say I look like Lucille Ball. But I wouldn't want to look like her. She's a screwball. How old are you?"

"I won't see fifty again," Norris said. "That's as far as I'm prepared to go."

"How old is she?"

Lottie laughed. "That's my little secret. Or we could say, I've forgotten, just as you forgot your last name." Bertha left.

"Did we hurt her feelings?" Norris said.

"She isn't taking in anything much. She's new here and makes the most terrible fusses. They may not let her stay in a semi-open ward if she doesn't begin to respond soon. Do you know, I'll have outside privileges next week? I'm quite looking forward to my first stroll around the block. And there's a gift shop in L 4. That's the main building."

"I know. I'm probably better acquainted with the exterior of the hospital than you are. Do the patients always have to go out in couples? It seems that way."

"Yes. If you're well enough to go out alone you're well enough to go home, the saying goes. I wonder if I'm going to take my old pleasure in housework when I go home? I'm quite spoiled here— making our own beds is the extent of it."

"Have you got plenty to read?"

"Lord yes. But I find I prefer fraternizing. It's part of the therapy here, mixing socially. And some patients like to talk out their problems. But I haven't reached that point and I doubt that I ever will. Once I've said 'I drank', I've told the whole story. Some of the patients come from quite complex family situations. Now I'm going to stop prattling right this minute. Tell me about you."

"Nothing to tell. Mrs Gompers leaves me my supper and I leave her the dishes. Then I watch a little TV or I read. I'm reading the new Agatha Christie right now—I don't think it's up to her level."

"Does it have Miss Marple in it?"

"No."

"Then I wouldn't care for it either, in all likelihood."

"Anyway, that's the story of my evening—and so to bed. After Deirdre's walk, that is."

"I miss her. Give her an extra biscuit and tell her it's from me." A different, older nurse paused in the door.

"Visiting hours are up," she said and moved on.

"I almost forgot," Norris said. He handed her a slip of paper. "These are people who called up to ask after you and sent their regards."

"Thoughtful," Lottie said, placing the paper on one side. "I'll walk to the outer door with you."

They found Bertha lying stretched across the corridor, face down and seemingly in a coma.

"Just step over her," Lottie said. "She's only doing it to attract attention. She wasn't doing well in college and, as they say, flipped out. Doubtless there's more to it than that. Well, here we are." She turned her cheek and Norris held his breath as he kissed her. "Don't forget tomorrow night—family group."

"Not likely to. It's good to see you looking yourself. Goodbye, peach."

2

In a room sparsely furnished with gleamingly polished bleached teak, Mag Carpenter was enjoying a dish of tea with Maureen Delahantey. From an adjoining room came the sounds of stilted conversation: Biddy was listening to her afternoon serials. Twing was curled up in a sunny chair, snoozing.

"The last time we were there," Maureen was saying, "she kept slipping out of the room. Tippling. But that was months ago."

"I know. A few weeks ago it seemed to me I hadn't heard from her in a moon's age. And it did seem odd—everyone had been so thoughtful, so attentive, since Bartram passed on. I thought, I'm going to take the bull by the horns and *I* am going to call *her*. So I did. This tea is scrumptious. Such a bouquet."

"It's something Irish. We order it special from New York because Biddy likes it."

"Anyhow, call her I did. And do you know, she could barely articulate! I said, 'Sounds to me like you're coming down with a cold.' Then there was a fearfully long pause with just her breathing. Heavily. Then she said, 'I don't think so.' The funny thing is, even then the thought never entered my mind. That she was drinking, I mean. But you know me, I'm the last one to see what's right under my nose. Is there any sugar?"

"Stupid me," Maureen said. The tea set matched the dinner ware, and was white and very plain. The pattern had once won a good design award.

"I wonder how Norris is taking it," Mag went on. "You know how he loves to tease, and I always say it's men like that who have the most sensitive feelings. The teasing is a cover up, you know, like an armadillo. I thought of having him over to supper but now that I'm single again I wasn't sure how it would look. She has enough on her mind, I imagine, without worrying about some widow setting her cap for her husband."

"You could have him along with some others. That's what I'm planning to do. I'm ashamed I haven't gotten to it yet."

A click came from the other room and Biddy joined them. "The Watsons are getting divorced. I've seen it coming for weeks."

"The Watsons?" Mag said.

"It's one of Biddy's serials. Which one is this? *A Town Called Pottsville?*"

"No. It's *Unto Each Day*. It takes place in a suburban town not unlike this one. Different families and the men going off to jobs in the city. Except the doctor. I don't know what Frank Watson sees in that secretary of his—she couldn't hoodwink me. Little schemer."

"I suppose they have to invent things," Mag said, "to keep the story going. Though a good deal of it is true enough to life, I imagine. Those things happen; and more besides."

"True enough," Biddy said. "A business associate of my father's went off with his stenographer. And took a good whack of the company capital with them. Luckily my father had a sharper eye than some credited him with. He followed the unhappy pair right to where they'd gone and got back the securities. Then he told the man he never wanted to see his face again. It was a very great scandal at the time. I'll just fetch myself a cup."

"I'll get it Biddy," Maureen said. "I want to make a fresh pot anyway. The boys will be in soon and they both like a cup of hot tea. Everyone in this family likes tea. Though Bryan prefers coffee in the morning."

"I don't feel like I'm out of bed yet until I've made my pot of coffee," Mag said. "There I am in my kitchen in my wrapper like a lump, waiting for it to perk. Then I can get down to things."

"I suppose you two," Biddy said, "have been reviewing the Mary Charlotte Taylor 'nervous breakdown' case." She gave a spry little laugh. "At least that's what it would have been called in my day. I'm happy to say there never were any of that kind of nerves in my family. We were brought up to think of drink as something common. None of us would have dreamed of touching a drop."

Maureen smiled. "It didn't exactly take with Bryan."

"You could never call Bryan a drinker, just because he likes a little something before dinner."

"Oh, I didn't mean he's a heavy drinker. I'd never stand for that," Maureen said.

"I confess I like my little glass of sherry before supper," Mag said. "I suppose that makes me a solitary drinker. I'll just have to face up to the burden, as I do my others. But I couldn't do without that little glass—Bartram and I made a ritual of it."

Maureen, who had gone to the kitchen, came back with a fresh pot of tea and a cup for Biddy. "What do you hear from Sonny and his family?" she asked.

"They adore California," Mag said. "And they send me color prints of the children quite regularly, so I feel in touch with their development. Baby Bartram is getting to be quite a big boy and can make letters. Not words, just letters. I'm planning to fly out for a short visit. I only wish they weren't quite so far off. They can't get away to come here—such a production with the children and little Debbie practically a babe in arms. It seems like yesterday that Sonny . . . but I musn't get started on that."

Patrick came in.

"Where's Michael?" Maureen asked.

Patrick shrugged. "Good afternoon, Mrs Carpenter."

"Are you two on the outs again?" Biddy asked. "I can always tell. You can't fool your old gran."

"Look at you," Mag said. "First you shot up like a bean pole, and now you've filled out."

"Why is your hair wet?" Biddy asked.

"I took a shower after practice. I always do."

"We never went out with wet hair. It's a wonder to me you all aren't dead of pneumonia. Then where would the football team be?"

"I'm sure it would take more than wet hair," Mag said, "to give a cold to anyone so in the pink of condition. Sonny never went in for football—track was his sport. Cross country running, in particular."

"I may go out for shot put. Michael is."

"This is news to me," Maureen said. "You know how your father feels about too much sport interfering with your studies."

"I do my studying at night. Can I have some tea?"

"May I," Biddy said. "It's such a simple distinction, I should think you could remember it."

"May I."

"Do you want a cup or a mug?" Maureen said.

"A mug. I'll take it up to my room. I've got a composition I've got to write. For English." Patrick fetched a mug, poured his tea, put in plenty of sugar and went upstairs.

"You must be very proud," Mag said, "two such fine stalwart sons."

"They're good boys," Biddy said, "and for the most part they get along like houses afire. Then they have these fallings out and won't speak to each other. Nobody knows why."

"If one of them uses something that belongs to the other," Maureen said, "that will do it."

(35)

"I sometimes felt quite guilty at having only one," Mag said. "An only child has special problems. But twins: I suppose you have to expect a special kind of sibling rivalry, from time to time."

"You do indeed," Maureen said. "More tea?"

3

It was family group night at the clinic. Doctor Kearney, a young man with red hair, was seated at the head of the long table. "I'm just here to audit," he said, "and put in my oar now and then. So whoever wants to get this off the ground, go ahead." A long silence ensued. "I take it no one has any problems worth discussing. I wonder if I couldn't spend my time in some more profitable way. Than just sitting here."

"There isn't a thing wrong with me," Mrs Brice said. "I was perfectly content with my home—I never was much for gadding about."

"You forget about the sleeping pills," her husband said. "You ought to tell them about that."

"It's not true that I tried to kill myself. I took some and I couldn't sleep so I took a couple more. What's wrong with that? The doctor prescribed them."

"One or two at bedtime," her husband said, "that's what it said on the bottle. You went into a coma."

"How long had you been taking sleeping pills?" Lottie asked in a kindly voice.

"What difference does it make," Mrs Brice said.

"You're picking on her," Bertha said. "Just like you all pick on me. Him most of all," she said, indicating the doctor. She was digging at the edge of the table, as though trying to gouge out a splinter.

"Do you feel we're picking on you, Mrs Brice?" Doctor Kearney asked.

"I guess not."

"Of course no one's picking on you," her husband said. "You slept very soundly all your life and then you started needing pills. You ought to talk about why, perhaps."

"What's to talk about? I couldn't sleep so the doctor gave me a prescription. You sound like I was some kind of dope addict. A person can't go night after night without getting any sleep. Sleep is something you've got to have, like food."

"Missing a night's sleep," Dr Kearney said, "won't kill anybody. You may feel shot the next day, but sooner or later you'll go to sleep."

"I didn't," Mrs Brice said.

"Perhaps you had something on your mind," Lottie said.

"And perhaps I didn't. Why is everybody talking about me? I'm not the only person here."

"You see?" Bertha said. "You are picking on her. The pills here stink. They just make you feel like a human vegetable. What I like is grass. I like to get high and meditate on the music. I *am* the music."

"Grass?" one of the patients, an older woman, said.

"Marijuana," Lottie said. "It's one of those psychedelic drugs you read about. It distorts reality."

"It's a lot better for you than booze," Bertha said. "I don't mind wine but I wouldn't want to be a big booze hound like some people."

"If you want to discuss my problem," Lottie said, "I'm willing. But I think we were getting some place with Mrs Brice, and ought to stick to the point. Wasn't there something that happened, that started your insomnia?"

Mrs Brice didn't answer.

"Why insist?" Norris said. "Obviously Mrs Brice isn't ready to talk about it yet."

"There's no time like the present," Dr Kearney said.

A long pause, and the atmosphere of the room became charged with tension. Bertha opened her mouth to speak, but Lottie said, "Shh." Mrs Brice put her head on the table and wept. "All killed, all killed," she said.

Mr Brice put his hand on his wife's shoulder. "There, there, Mother," he said.

Bertha became rigid and slid out of her chair and under the table. The thump of her head was softened by her heavy hair.

"Oh I don't like this," the wife of one of the patients said. "Can't you do something for her? Can't you give her an injection?"

"Bertha is on her own medication regimen," Dr Kearney said. "And if she keeps pulling stunts like this she won't stay long in an open ward. She disturbs the other patients."

"She doesn't disturb me," Lottie said. "If Bertha likes to lie on the floor, why not? She's seemed much improved these last few days."

Mrs Brice raised her head and her husband gave her his handkerchief, with which she dried her cheeks.

"It was the shock," Mr Brice said. "Fanny hasn't been herself since the funeral. I thought she would come out of it gradually, but . . ."

"Don't talk about it," Mrs Brice said. "It's over and done with and I haven't anything left. What business of theirs is it, anyway?"

"That's the way I feel," another patient said. "I have to stay here for three months but that doesn't mean anybody's going to force me to talk about my private business."

"Who's forcing you, Mr Mulwin?" Dr Kearney asked.

"You are," said Mr Mulwin.

"I wasn't aware of it."

"That's one of your tricks to get me to talk. Well, I won't."

"You don't have to talk," his wife said, "until you're ready to. This is a kind of open meeting. People realize other people have problems too. I can see how it helps."

"Another county heard from," Mr Mulwin said.

"If you won't talk, maybe I will," his wife said.

"You never could keep your trap shut, could you."

Mrs Brice put her head on the table and began to sob again.

"That's right, Mother, let it out."

Under the table Bertha groaned. "I'm sick," she said.

"You sure aren't going to get well down there," Dr Kearney said.

"Why don't you join the rest of us?" Lottie asked.

"I'm going to vomit," Bertha said.

A nurse, who had been sitting in a corner of the room taking notes, put down her notebook and got up. She moved Bertha's chair out of the way, hauled Bertha out into the open, hoisted her to her feet and half led, half dragged her from the room. Bertha was making retching noises.

(38)

"It isn't all acting," Lottie said. "She looks awful."

"Acting," Mr Mulwin said. "You're pretty good at that yourself. You act like you're some kind of head woman around here. So helpful. Always a kind word. Florence Nightingale."

"My wife is making a serious effort to recover from a particular illness. Your sarcasm is no help," Norris said.

"Like me to punch your head?" Mr Mulwin offered.

"Certainly not. Your aggressiveness is merely a symptom of whatever is ailing you, and whether you get well is a matter of profound indifference to me."

"It better be, because it's none of your damn business."

"Oh Greg," Mrs Mulwin said, "why do you talk so? You never hit anybody in your life."

"There's always a first time."

"Please understand," Norris said, "I am not trying to pick a fight with you. But I'd like you to show my wife the respect due to a lady."

"I'll make a deal with you: I won't speak to her at all. The pleasure will be all mine."

"Oh Greg," Mrs Mulwin said.

"And you can stop, 'Oh Greging'. I've got a business that's going to pot while I'm stuck in this boy scout camp or whatever it is."

"Violence," Mrs Brice said, raising her head, "I don't like it. Mr Brice has never raised his voice to me in all the years of our marriage."

"Of course not, Mother. You're a good kind woman. I think some women who get shouted at·provoke it themselves. You know, women who nag, and things like that. Here, use my hankie."

"Was that a crack at me?" Mrs Mulwin asked.

"For goodness sake, no," Mr Brice said. "I was speaking in general."

"If I ever did nag Greg, it was for his own good. He hates getting up in the morning, but if he's late for work, it puts him in a mood. He's very scrupulous about his business."

"Will you shut up?" queried Mr Mulwin. "If I get in a mood, it's because I've got things on my mind."

"If you got some of them off your mind," Lottie said, "you might not be so disaggreeable. Feel so disagreeable on the inside, I mean."

"Am I supposed to take that lying down?" Mr Mulwin asked Norris.

"No," Norris said, "sitting up."

"I'm not one bit used to all this wrangling," Mrs Brice said. "I like peace and quiet in which to think my thoughts. If I promise not to take any more sleeping pills can I go to my own home?"

"Now dear," Mr Brice said, "you know you can't leave until the three months are up. That was one of the conditions on which I signed you into this fine hospital."

"I'm not used to sleeping in the same room with three other women. I'm used to privacy and my own things."

"How have you been sleeping, Mrs Brice?" Dr Kearney asked.

"All right. I wake up in the night but after a while I go back to sleep. Everybody does that, I guess."

"I'm thinking of taking you off your night medication," the doctor said. "I think you can get along without it."

"Please don't do that," Mrs Brice said. "One of the ladies in my room is a heavy snorer and I know I won't get a wink of sleep. If I don't get my sleep, I feel dreadful."

"I understand how you feel," Lottie said. "I live in fear and trembling of having my medication changed. I don't care if it does make me smell like a hearse."

"It will be changed," the doctor said, "soon enough. You'll have to anticipate a certain discomfort in making the adjustment."

Mr Mulwin chuckled. Norris gave him a quelling look and Mr Mulwin stuck out his tongue at him.

"That," his wife said, "is childish."

Chapter III

1

The phone rang. As always when this happened, Deirdre put back her head and howled. Norris answered it.

"Norris? How are you. This is Mag—Mag Carpenter."

"Good to hear from you Mag. I'm fine. So is Deirdre." With his free hand he scratched the proud dog behind its ear.

"Now I want you to tell me all about Lottie. I'm sure she's doing wonderfully. A person like that, with so many inner resources and such a strong character. I've often said it, Mary Charlotte Taylor is an oak."

Norris, who did not much like Mag, said to himself, Go soak your head. Aloud he said, "She's doing just fine. It's quite a set-up they've got there. It's not just a rest home—they have a lot of group therapy."

"Group therapy, I've heard about that. But I'd die before I could start talking about all my little intimacies in front of strangers. I simply couldn't face it."

"It is hard on some people, at first. You know, they have certain nights when the families come and join in. It helps the patients realize that they're not ostracized from the community."

"Yes. And of course most problems aren't just one person's. I mean, so often it seems in an emotional upset the other members of the family are in some way involved too. Oh dear, I'm making it sound as though you drove Lottie to drink. I don't mean that, of course."

"Who knows?" Norris said. "Maybe I did." He stopped scratching Deirdre and reached for the highball he allowed himself after dinner. "Although Lottie says she wants me to keep on having my usual when she comes home. I think she sees it as sort of a test, and one that it's important she pass."

"Norris, I'd like to ask you a rather personal question."

"Oh?"

"Would you like to come over and spend the night with me?"

"I'm flattered that you should ask me that. It's a real compliment. But I think we'd better not."

"I don't know what possessed me to say that—I just blurted it out. That wasn't why I called up. Truly, seriously."

"I can understand that you're lonely, Mag."

"I guess it's a way of missing Bartram. We had a very satisfying relationship. At the same time, I really like the idea of remaining faithful to his memory. Promise me you won't breathe it to a soul, especially Lottie. I couldn't look her in the face if I thought she knew."

"No, I regard it as a confidence. And I think you'll feel better for getting it off your chest. Sometimes saying a thing is enough. And I am flattered."

"You should be. You're the only one I ever said anything like that to. You're a very attractive man, Norris. That silvery hair."

"And you're an attractive, pretty woman, Mag. I've always thought that. But don't worry. We'll call this our little secret."

"I know I can count on you. I'm thinking of giving a little dinner party, or perhaps have cocktails. I'll invite you."

"I'll be happy to come. Unless it's one of the nights when I go to the hospital."

(42)

"I'll arrange it so it isn't. Remember me to Lottie. Tell her I'll come see her when she can have visitors."

"Will do. Goodnight Mag, and thanks for calling."

"Goodbye Norris. Don't forget: It's our little secret."

After Norris finished his highball and took Deirdre for her walk he called Mag back.

"Mag? It's Norris. Is that invitation still open?"

"Yes, Norris. It is."

"It will take me half an hour or so to walk over there. The car would be too conspicuous."

"I'll be expecting you."

When he got to the Carpenter house the porch light was off and the downstairs dark. The door opened before he could ring the bell. He could see Mag by the dim light that filtered down the staircase from the upper hall. She was wearing a flowered housecoat. Norris took her in his arms and kissed her.

"I've never been to bed with any woman but Lottie," he said.

"Hush," Mag said. "Don't talk." She took him by the hand and led him upstairs to her room, which was done in rose and pale blue, dominated by a reproduction mahogany four poster. "I fixed us a couple of drinks." Two highballs stood on the dresser. "May I watch you undress?"

Afterward, Norris said, "I'd like to spend the night. But I don't think it would look too good for the neighbors to see me issuing forth while they're crouched over their Rice Crispies. It might look a little *too* good."

"I know," Mag said. She lay very close to him, with one leg over his. "I know this is going to sound sordid, but perhaps sometime we could meet at a motel. Then we could spend the whole night together."

"Lottie won't be away long. We don't want to start something that might be difficult to handle, later."

"Oh, I won't make any claims on you. It's just that I'd like to wake up once more and find a man's body next to mine."

"Any man's body?"

"That's nasty. I meant your body, Norris. It was so wonderful:

(43)

don't say anything that will make it seem squalid. I couldn't bear that."

Norris kissed her lightly. "I was only teasing. But I'd better warn you: I'm an independent cuss."

"I know you are. That's one of the things I like about you."

"And now, I'll get a move on."

"Norris?"

"Yes?"

"Could you do it again?"

"Sorry, Mag, but I've never been able to manage that. Put on the light. I've got to hustle my bustle."

2

Biddy was in the kitchen, rustling up an apple pie when Michael came in.

"Where's Patrick?" he said.

"I heard one of you come in and go upstairs, then come down and go out again. It must have been Patrick, if it wasn't you. Tramp, tramp. What a pair of elephants. The whole house shakes."

"He took my track shoes without asking. Not that I would have let him if he had asked. He's too lazy to get his own fixed."

"Are you sure you looked carefully? You boys are always misplacing things. Did you look under your bed?"

"Yes. Anyway, I don't keep them under the bed. I keep them in my closet. I'm going to get even with him for this."

Maureen came in from shopping. "I'm glad to see you," she said to Michael. "You can bring in the bundles from the car. My back is aching just from loading them in."

"I've got to go down to the field."

"You don't 'got to' anything until those bundles are brought in. Now do it and no more back talk." Michael went sullenly about his task.

"He says Patrick took his track shoes," Biddy said. "I'm sure he just borrowed them, thinking Michael wouldn't be using them to-

(44)

day."

"That's all I need: more friction between those two. Sometimes I wish I'd had a little boy and then a little girl, instead of twins. Life would be so much easier."

"What a thing to say, you surprise me, Maureen. You know you wouldn't sacrifice one of your twins."

Maureen laughed. "Oh, I'm not planning any human sacrifices. Though I admit I'm sometimes tempted. I need tea."

Michael came in, trying to carry too many bags at once. One of them tore and fell. A gush of milk issued from it. Maureen said, "Oh!", only it was more of a scream.

"Clumsy, you can clean that up, then you can get on your bike and go buy another container of milk."

"I didn't do it on purpose. I've got to go down to the field: the coach expects me."

"I can mop up the milk," Biddy said. "It won't take me a minute."

"No, Biddy. Michael has to learn sometime. He's going to finish unloading the car, mop up and go to the store. That's that."

"Good gosh," Michael said. "Just because Patrick sneaks in and out of the house . . . "

"I said, that's that."

"Good grief," Michael said. He did as he was bidden.

When he had gone off on his bike, Maureen sat down with a cup of tea at the table where Biddy was deftly handling her pie dough. "It was the funniest thing," Maureen said, "at the supermarket. Mag Carpenter was there and I'm just as certain as I'm sitting here that she saw me. But she suddenly wheeled her cart around and went skittering off down another aisle. I'd swear she was avoiding me. Of course when I saw how the land lay, I did not give chase."

"That is funny," Biddy said. "Mag is always the first to make the overtures. She's such a cheery little bird, she reminds me of a robin redbreast. Or perhaps more of a chickadee—you know the way she sort of cheeps when she talks. All those little laughs."

"And smothered giggles. That was what was so odd. It wasn't at all like her."

"Maybe she was minded of something she forgot, and didn't see

(45)

you."

"Maybe. But I don't think so: our eyes met."

"Probably she needs spectacles. Many people hold out against getting them. Vanity. She looks younger than she must be and spectacles do make a person look older."

"Mag is older than I am," Maureen said, "and I think she looks it. Today she seemed almost haggard."

"I find that hard to picture, Mag Carpenter looking haggard. She's borne up so well since Bartram passed on. And she always puts in such a nice appearance, she must have quite a wardrobe. But Bartram must have left her nicely off. It was my understanding that that business of his did quite nicely, thank you. He was never one for throwing his money around."

"You can say that again. I'll never to my dying day forget the time I went there collecting for multiple sclerosis. He gave me some song and dance about their charities, and how they'd already subscribed all they were going to for the year. Can you imagine? Five dollars! Which was certainly the most I expected from Bartram Carpenter. I'll wager he put buttons in the collection bag at church."

"One of my brothers did that once. Walter. But he only did it once, I'll tell you. The man reached into the bag, fished it out and handed it back to Walter. Oh, there was a to-do when we got back from church that Sunday."

Patrick came in.

"Your brother says you took his track shoes," Maureen said.

"I only borrowed them. He wasn't using them."

"You know what the rule is about taking each other's things without asking first. What's wrong with your track shoes? They're practically brand-new."

"The stiching came out of one of them. They have to go to the shoemaker's."

"No time like the present," Biddy said.

"I'm tired. What kind of pie is that, Gran?"

"Ask me no questions and I'll tell you no lies."

"It's apple. I can smell it."

"You can have a cup of tea," Maureen said, "then you're going to

(46)

take those shoes to the shoemaker. If you ask him nicely, he may get them ready for you tomorrow. But you're not to touch Michael's again, is that clear?"

"Has he been whining around about it? What a tattle-tale. You'd think he'd grow up and talk to me about it, man-to-man."

"How was school?" Biddy asked. "Is that French teacher still down on you?"

"What a subject. It's not my fault if my accent sounds like pig-Latin."

"You ought to try, Maureen"

"I *do* try. *Où est la plume de ma tante?*"

"*Sur la table,*" Biddy said. "It must run in the family. Bryan couldn't make head or tail of languages, and he had to pass two to get into college. I was an A scholar in French myself. I've forgotten it all now. Sometimes I wish I'd kept it up, though I don't know what the use would be."

"Frankly, French bored me silly," Maureen said. "It was partly the teacher. I can't think what her name was, but she was a true old maid of the old fashioned school. She wore her hair in a pompadour brushed up over a rat. She couldn't keep order in the class room and I'm ashamed to say we took all kinds of advantage of her. I used to sit and draw in my notebook and pass notes to the other girls. How unkind children are."

"I don't see why I have to keep hammering away at French," Patrick said. "I don't know that I want to go to college."

"Just see," Maureen said, "that you don't say that in front of your father."

3

"Why yes," Mrs. Brice said, "a game of bridge might be nice. Today would have been my son's thirty-seventh birthday, if he had lived."

"What a sad memorial," Lottie said, "and how kind of you to tell me. I'd ask Mr Mulwin to make a fourth, only I'm afraid he'd bite my head off. I think I'll just risk it." She crossed the sun room to the settee where Mr Mulwin was perusing a magazine. "Oh Mr Mulwin," she said in a bright voice, "we're getting up a foursome for bridge. Would you care to join us?"

"Don't play bridge," he said, barely glancing up. "Thanks anyway," he added grudgingly.

"Perhaps you'd like to learn. We're all very amateur. It's just to pass the time, you know. Or we could try Monopoly or Scrabble."

"No games," Mr Mulwin said. "Now if you'll excuse me, I'm trying to think about my business. Just because I'm locked in here doesn't mean I can't telephone the office and keep an eye on things."

"But you're here for a rest, to get you mind *off* things," said the indomitable Lottie.

"Now look, Mrs Taylor, I don't want to be rude, but in a word, bug off."

Lottie turned on her heel and returned to Mrs Brice. "Well, he didn't exactly bite my head *all* the way off. It looks like it will have to be gin rummy."

"Gin rummy?" Mrs Brice said. "I don't know how to play that."

"I'll teach you."

"I'm not sure that's such a good idea: it might confuse my bridge. I'm just beginning to grasp that."

"Did you make those moccasins in craft therapy?" They were assembled of ready cut pieces, decorated with a few beads and were very ugly.

"Why yes, I did. To my great surprise. I've never been a bit handy. I don't know why you take such an interest in me. It's kindly of you to bother. My son's name was Theodore, but he was always and only called Thad. His children's names were Debbie, Peter and Baby Sam. His wife's name was Marie. It happened on the Labor Day weekend." Mrs Brice lapsed into silence, and Lottie found herself at a loss for something to say.

Finally she said, "I have a cousin named Theodore, but we've always called him Ted. He's rather a rascal, quite the wit and one for the ladies. He's never married. At his age I imagine he's beginning to quiet down a little now."

Bertha wandered in and joined them. "Is this a sun room or a solarium?" she asked in a truculent voice. "I call it the sun room, but that male nurse just drove me off my bed and said go sit in the 'solarium.' I like a thing to be called one thing or the other." It was pouring out. "Sun room," she added bitterly.

"I suppose," Lottie said, "they don't like us to lie on our beds in the daytime for fear we won't sleep at night. Then, too, they believe in socializing."

"Sitting around gabbing."

"That's a pretty dress, Bertha," Mrs Brice said.

"I'm going to play the phonograph," Bertha said. "Liven this dump up."

"Please don't turn the volume *too* high," Lottie said.

"I like to be able to hear it," Bertha said. She went to the phonograph at the end of the room and put on a record which had been popular the year before. She began to do a sort of shuffling dance by herself.

"I'm glad she's stopped lying around on the floor," Mrs Brice said. "I used to find it so worrying, that somebody was that sick."

Bertha went over to Mr Mulwin and said, "Will you dance with me?"

"No."

"Why not?"

"I don't want to. Besides, I don't know how."

"Come on, I'll teach you. All you have to do is move around to the music."

"What's with this everybody trying to teach me something? Now you're a nice girl, Bertha, but I wish you'd run along." Bertha shrugged and went back to her shuffling.

"I hope they let me see the hairdresser soon," Mrs Brice said. "I'm a sight."

"Would you like me to give you a shampoo," Lottie offered, "and a set? I'm quite good at it. Your hair takes a very nice wave."

"You have a visitor," a nurse announced. Lottie looked beyond her. Mag Carpenter stood in the doorway, her head cocked on one side, and smiling her little smile. She wore a smart rain outfit and carried a furled English umbrella.

"Isn't this a surprise," Lottie said, "and such a nice one. How brave, on a day like this. Mrs Brice, Mrs Carpenter."

Mrs Brice gave a rather mumbled, "Very pleased to meet you I'm sure," and scurried off.

"I'm going to be perfectly truthful," Mag said. "I had to drive out this way, and I thought, I'm just going to pop in and find out if I can't see Lottie, I'm tired of waiting to hear whether she can have visitors. You know what a creature of impulse I am, so I did it and here I am. The nurse couldn't have been sweeter about letting me in: you seem quite a pet of hers."

"Here I am," Lottie said, "in our so-called sun room." She indicated the steaming windows which gave off a chilly draught. "Come to my room and take off your things. We can have a little chat in private."

Mag looked restlessly around. "It seems quite pleasant here, and I can only stay a minute. We could sit over there." She indicated two chairs by the coffee urn. "Do you suppose I might have a cup of that? Or is it off-limits to visitors?"

"But of course, though I won't vouch for it as much of a treat. Still, it is hot." She filled two paper cups with the not unnoxious brew and the women seated themselves.

"Now bring me up to date on all I've been missing," Lottie said.

"I don't think there's a thing to tell. The town has been as quiet as a dormouse. The League of Women Voters had a rather stormy session, but it all blew over. And Biddy Delahantey had a fall. They were quite alarmed that she might have broken her hip, and you know what that would mean at her age. But she was only badly bruised, and, of course, shaken. I believe she's up and about already. Now there's a spirited creature for you."

"Yes. An inspiration . . ."

"Hello." It was Norris. He had on a raincoat and carried a wet fedora. "How are you Mag? Lottie, I know, is fine." He bent and kissed her cheek.

"Why Norris," Mag said. "What a treat, getting to see both of you at once. Quite like the old days." She was discomposed.

(50)

"I didn't expect you dear," Lottie said. "You needn't have, not on a day like this."

Norris shrugged. "A short dash from the car . . ."

"You must take a hot shower when you get home, and make yourself a toddy. This is just the wrong time of year to take a chill."

"Heavens!" Mag said. "I had no idea it was so late. Is that really the time? Lottie, I'm going to come back and pay you a real visit, and not be such a creature of impulse. I'll plan ahead and let you know. Nice to see you, Norris." And she left before the Taylors could make their goodbyes.

"That was pretty funny," Lottie said.

"What was?" Norris asked.

"She barely got here and off she goes like a shot. She never even touched the coffee she asked for. From my experience here, I'd say she's under a nervous strain."

"The after effects of Bartram's death may be catching up with her. A widow, alone in a big house."

"Could be. She always had a fliberty-gibbet side to her. I think she thinks it becomes her, but I'm not at all sure it does."

Norris laughed. "More to be pitied than censured."

"Who's censuring her? She has all my sympathy. But sometimes the people from the outside who come here seem more rattled and gaga than the ones on the inside."

Bertha approached. "I know you," she said. "You're her husband."

"That's right. I'm Norris Taylor, and you are Bertha. We've met before."

"You're the one who thinks I look like Elizabeth Taylor. Is she related to you?"

"No. I believe the famous actress is of an English family. Though doubtless all Taylors are cousins in some remote degree."

"Then you are related to her."

"Possibly. All men are kin."

"You're no kin of mine," Bertha said. She wandered away again, doubtless in hopes of evading the nurse and sneaking in a cat-nap.

Chapter IV

1

"It looks like we're very much the winners, Norris," Mag said. She was totting up a bridge score.

"You're lucky we were only playing for a quarter a corner," Norris said.

"Would have wiped me out," Bryan said, "completely. Now what is it?" Patrick had entered the living room.

"I can't find my biology review book. It's gray."

"Would anyone care for a drink?" Maureen asked.

"I wouldn't mind a scotch and soda," Mag said. "Very weak on the scotch and heavy on the soda."

"I'll buy one of those," Norris said.

"Look under the sofa," Biddy said to Patrick. "Twing may have taken it to play with. I hunted and hunted today for my maroon wool, and there I finally found it, under the sofa. That cat. And once I got down and got it, I thought I'd never straighten up again. They'll find me here, I thought, and think I've gone crazy, trying to crawl under the furniture." She was seated in an Eames chair, crocheting.

"You should have asked me to look, Biddy," Maureen said, "after your fall."

"He doesn't play with books," Patrick said. "Just fluffy things, like sweaters."

"Biology," Mag said, "that's an interesting subject."

"Borrow Michael's," Bryan said, "while he's studying something else. And stop losing things. You wouldn't know where to find your head if it wasn't screwed on."

"He's using his and I've got to find mine. We have a test tomorrow."

"You may have left it in your locker at school," Biddy said. "It's easy to overlook things."

"No. I know I had it. I think Michael hid it, to get even."

"To get even for what?" Bryan asked.

"Oh, there was some fuss about some track shoes," Maureen said, "but that's past history."

"I'll just go up and look into this," Bryan said.

"No," Maureen said. "I'll go. You mix the drinks. And I'd like a small brandy. And you might put the kettle on for Biddy's chamomile tea."

"Shall I wash the dishes and mop the floor while I'm at it?"

"If you wish." Maureen and Patrick left the room. In the boys' room the gray review book conspicuously topped Patrick's other school books on his desk.

"I knew you hid it," Patrick said.

"Hid what?" Michael was all innocence.

"I have half a mind to tell your father about this, Michael," Maureen said. "You're not too big for a good strapping."

Michael flushed deeply. "He better not hit me."

"Mouth," Maureen said. "Don't talk in that fresh way to your mother, or the second the company's gone I'll tell him about it and then we'll see. Now I want you boys to apologize to each other and shake hands."

The boys glowered at each other, then Patrick extended his hand, which Michael took.

(54)

"I'm sorry about the track shoes. Honest, I didn't think you were using them that day."

"That's OK."

"Now, with your permission, may I rejoin my guests?" Maureen said, and left the room.

"Creep," Michael said.

"Double sucks with balls on," Patrick said. "Now let me study. I know I'm going to flunk this crazy test."

"Wouldn't surprise me," Michael said. "You are pretty dumb."

"Come on: truce."

"OK. Truce. Now that I got even for the track shoes."

Downstairs, Bryan had made and brought in the drinks. He was reviewing the bridge score. "What's this giant figure?" he asked.

"That's our little slam in hearts, which you doubled and I redoubled. Don't tell me you've forgotten," Mag said.

"If I were Bryan, I'd want to forget," Norris said. "But even without that big bonanza, we had you trounced." He picked up a quarter from Bryan's corner of the table. "Don't forget your winnings, Mag."

Bryan tossed down the score pad. "The trouble," Maureen said, "is that Bryan can't bear not to play every hand. So he consistently overbids."

"Overbids! With the cards I held tonight? Did you settle that matter with the twins?"

"Yes. It was a tempest in a teapot. Michael was teasing Patrick, but they're on the best of terms now."

Bryan made a sound usually rendered as "humph."

"Do you know, son," Biddy said, "I think Michael is taller than you are now? I was noticing it when we were standing around the table, saying grace. Patrick probably is, too, only he slouches so. All boys that age do. Big boys, that is. Sometimes I'd like to give him a good shake and say, 'Stand up straight. Be proud of your height.' There were never any short men in my father's family. On my mother's side the men tended to be more just average. In height and every other way. Mother was the bright spot in that family."

"So long as they don't get too big for their britches," Bryan said.

(55)

"Which I sometimes think they are. We'll be going into that if their report cards don't improve."

"It's Patrick who's the poorer scholar," Maureen said. "Michael does quite well. I wish you wouldn't go on about it so. It makes Patrick feel inferior, and then there's friction."

"You're a fine one to talk, Bryan," his mother said. "You were must the same at their age: all sports and no study. It's a miracle to me how you ever got into Cornell."

"Did I understand you to say they're both going in for the decathlon at the state meet?" Norris said. "They must be fine athletes to qualify for that."

"They'll never make it on the track," Bryan said. "Too heavy. Though Michael might just: he's the lighter of the two."

"Neither of them is a feather," Biddy said. "Food! How they eat! I love to see them stow it away."

"Our food bills," Maureen said, "are simply awesome."

"Decathlon," Mag said, "is that something at the Olympics?"

"Any big sporting event," Norris said, "might have a decathlon. You have to qualify in a number of events, running, shot-put, and so on."

"Sports," Mag said. "Tennis and swimming are the beginning and end of it for me. And I've never progressed beyond the breaststroke. I don't like having my head in the water."

"Field hockey was the alpha and omega of sports for me," Maureen said. "Once a girl from another school hacked my shins on purpose. Don't think I didn't get my own back. It broke the skin. I could never understand taking games so seriously."

"In my day," Biddy said, "serious athletics for girls were undreamt of. We did Swedish calesthenics. I was quite good at twirling the Indian clubs. Some of the movements were very graceful. I wonder why they went out of style? They weren't so competitive, which was nice." She was adding a scalloped border to the throw she had crocheted. Biddy's Christmas offerings were as predictable as her tireless hook, and some friends felt decidedly over-stocked.

"Competitive sports," Bryan said, "make a man of a boy. They prepare him for later life, for the give and take and the hurley-burley."

"You might say, they sort the men from the boys," Norris said.

"Do you mean that?" Bryan asked, "or is that one of your sarcasms?"

"It could be both," Norris said. "I wasn't much of an athlete, so I have to stick up for the underdog."

"You ought to take up golf."

"As the saying goes, thanks but no thanks."

"Norris always looks trim," Mag said. "Do you go in for any particular exercise?"

"Just a little gardening. A very little gardening."

"I thought you had a yardman," Maureen said, "who came in and did that."

"We do. But Lottie doesn't trust him around the roses. No more do I, for the matter of that."

"Roses," Biddy said, "the queen of flowers." She shook out the crocheted maroon throw, so all could see it. "Isn't this just the color of an American Beauty?" It wasn't, but if anyone knew it, no one said it.

"Any refills?" Bryan asked.

"Heavenly days," Mag said, "not for me. I have no head for it: two and I'm squiffy. I wouldn't have had one, if I had to drive. It was so good of Norris to drive way out of his way and pick me up, when my car wouldn't start."

"Did you look at the engine?" Bryan asked Norris.

"Not my job."

"Oh I'm probably just out of gas," Mag said. "It wouldn't be the first time. You know what a forgetter I am. Norris, if it's all right with you, I think it's nearly my beddy-bye time."

In the car Norris said, "Mag, was it true your car wouldn't start?"

"It was a white lie. Perhaps it won't start: I didn't try it. Can you come in for a little while?"

"No, I can't. And I'm annoyed with you about this. It's important that we not do anything to make us conspicuous."

"Please don't be, Norris dear. Besides, why shouldn't my car not start? It happens all the time."

"You ought to have your car overhauled."

"I didn't mean it happens to *my* car all the time. People's. You're not being very nice to me this evening."

"Either we stick to our plans without any hanky-panky about stalled engines, or all deals are off. I'm very fond of you, Mag, or we wouldn't be where we are, but Maureen Delahantey is a very noticing sort of a person, and I won't have Lottie upset. She's never going to know about this."

"I said before that I understood that. I'm sorry if I was naughty—just this once. But it was fun, having you drive over to pick me up."

In the Delehantey's bedroom Maureen, who was brushing her dark lustrous hair, said, "Did you notice, during the bidding, that at one point Mag started to call Norris Bartram?"

"So?" Bryan was laying out his clothes for the morning. He was a careful dresser.

"It struck me as funny."

"What's so funny about it? I suppose all her life she's been used to having Bartram as her bridge partner. Seems natural enough to me."

"It wasn't so much that, as the way she caught herself and looked when she said it. She seemed to try to hide what she'd said, if you know what I mean."

Bryan gave his rich laugh. "One thing I know," he said, "is that I do not see Norris Taylor as the heavy lover. In fact, I wonder if he's still able to do justice to that juicy wife of his." Maureen was sitting in her slip, and he gave her shoulder a love pinch that made her squeal.

Down the hall, in the twins room, things were not going too well. Michael was in his brother's bed, but Patrick had moved up his heavy thigh and covered his parts. Michael tried to get his hand underneath, but couldn't.

"I'm trying to sleep," Patrick said, in a pretend-asleep voice.

"Come on," Michael muttered.

"Go way."

"No."

"We're supposed to be in training," Patrick said.

"Don't be a jerk," Michael said. "The book says all that stuff about an orgasm making you weak is a lot of hooey."

There was a light rap. Michael was back in his own bed, quick and quiet as a wink.

"Are you boys talking in there?" It was Biddy.

"Hunh?" Michael said. What's that Gran?"

"Well, just don't let your parents hear you talking. It's late enough, in all conscience."

2

"I imagine most of you have met our new guest, Mrs Judson," Dr Kearney said to the group assembled around the table. Those who had not, introduced themselves. Mrs Judson was a thin woman in the midst of life—an unhappy one, judging by the drawn expression of her face. Her husband, a portly man, was seated a little to her left and behind her.

"I'm Sam Judson," he said. "Just call me Sam, everybody does. Sam Judson used cars and rentals, it's not above three blocks from here."

"Why Norris," Lottie said, "we once rented a car from Mr Judson, the time we had all that trouble with the old Dodge. How fortuitous."

"Yes," Norris said. "I remember. A fine car, as I recall it."

"No rental from Sam Judson's will ever give you any trouble. We pride ourselves on that. But I'm not here tonight to promote business, so I won't give you the sales pitch."

Mrs Judson sighed. "What is it we're supposed to do?" she asked of no one in particular.

Lottie shivered nervously. "We talk," she said. There was silence, then Mrs Brice spoke.

"I haven't had any night medication for two nights now. No, it's three. I slept pretty well, considering."

"Sounds like progress to me," Dr Kearney said. He gave her a smile.

"Can I go home?" Mrs Brice asked.

"We've gone into that before, Mother," Mr Brice said. "Not yet a while."

"I wonder, doctor," Lottie said, "if you haven't changed my medication too soon. I feel so apprehensive all the time."

"You're experiencing discomfort, I take it," Dr Kearney said.

"No, it's more than discomfort. I feel apprehensive, I feel anxious, I feel as though something horrible is going to happen, and it's right inside my head. This afternoon I would have given my hope of heaven for a drink—a good stiff glass of vodka. Or gin. Anything."

"I wouldn't mind a stiff drink myself," Mr Mulwin said. "And I'm going to have one when I get out of here. Alcohol is no problem for me."

"It could get to be one," his wife said, "if you don't take it easy."

"You said that on purpose to torment me," Lottie said to Mr Mulwin. "Why are you so hateful all the time?" Norris patted her arm. Lottie was kneading her hands in her lap.

"He was only bragging," Mrs Mulwin said. "It's a way some men have, and he's one of them."

"Why do you come to these sessions?" Mr Mulwin asked his wife. "You only stir me up."

"Lately everything stirred you up. That's why you're here."

"I'm not stirred up either," Mrs Judson said. "I don't know what I'm doing here."

"Problems," Mr Brice said. "Perhaps you're a little like Mrs Brice here—withdrawn, I think they call it."

"I *know*," Lottie said, "there must be some medication you could give me that would help me through this ghastly period."

"We'll talk that over," Dr Kearney said, "in your private session."

"But that's not until tomorrow. Oh Norris, they're torturing me."

"Oh dear," Mrs Brice said, "I don't like to see you like this: you're such a kindly, collected person. I'm sure they're only trying to do what's right."

"It's not enough. I'm the one who knows how I feel."

"I don't want to get like her," Mrs Judson said. "Take me home, Sam. I've changed my mind."

"Don't worry," Bertha said, "you won't get like her. She's an alcoholic, though what that's a symptom of, who knows? Change of life is my guess. You have some other problem. My problem is acting freaky. I just wanted to be myself, play my records, stay up all night, it wasn't anything wrong. But the other students couldn't bear it. My own roommate moved out on me."

"You're damn right I'm an alcoholic," Lottie said, "I think I always will be. But that doesn't mean I'm going to take any lip from you, Bertha."

"This is an open session, I can say what I like."

"Why is it, then, *your* family never comes to these evenings?"

"Because they freak me out, I have fits when I see my family." Bertha became rigid. "I'd like to scream my head off at you, you phoney. Whited sepulchre."

"Do I have to put up with this, Dr Kearney?" Lottie demanded.

"Leave me out of it," the doctor said. "The quarrel is between you ladies."

"Piss, fuck, shit," Bertha chanted.

"Sam," Mrs Judson said, "I don't like it here a bit. I told you, I've changed my mind."

"We talked that all out at home, Ethel. You said you could see yourself that you needed help. You did make suicide threats, you know, and that wasn't like you."

"You don't have to tell the whole world," Mrs Judson said.

"Mrs Judson," Mrs Brice said, "I understand so well how you feel. I often find these sessions distressing—people saying things right out in the open, and all the quarreling and disagreeableness. I've never cared a whit for anything disagreeable—it's so unnecessary. I don't see why we can't talk things over sensibly, if there is anything to talk over."

"You see?" Mr Brice said, "bringing things out in the open does seem to help. When you first came here you wouldn't say a word, just sit and look forlorn, like at home."

"Doesn't my hair look nice? Lottie Taylor gave me a shampoo and set today, even though she was feeling terribly nervous."

"It's more than nervous," Lottie said.

"But you find you can function," Dr Kearney said, "despite the discomfort you're experiencing."

(61)

"Function, of course I can function. I could function if I had a broken leg, but that doesn't mean I'm going to go leaping off a ski jump. Part of what upsets me is that I know you have medication that will make this transition more bearable for me. It's cruel, it's sadistic."

"I think you're doing very well. Make an effort to relax, and as I said, we'll discuss this in our private session tomorrow."

"Tomorrow! Oh God how long. A whole night and a morning to get through. I wish I had just gone on drinking until I died."

"I can ski," Bertha said.

"No, Lottie," Norris said, "that's not true. It was your idea as much as mine that you come here. You saw that you needed it, and you did it."

"Why do you always sit there," Mr Mulwin asked Norris, "with that wise old owl look on your face? You think you're the cat's meow, don't you."

"Your own mug," Norris said, "is not precisely a garland of roses. Your petulant truculence shows in it very plainly. It looks puerile, which means childish, in the event you don't know."

"Aren't we descending to personalities?" Sam Judson asked. "I don't see what Mrs Judson is going to get out of these kind of goings on."

"Oh, now you're trying to get in on the act, buster," Mr Mulwin said.

"For Pete's sake," said Mrs Mulwin, "be yourself. Or stop being yourself and be the self you used to be. All this bullying talk is just a cover up for the things you really want to talk about, only you won't let them out. I'm not so dumb as you think I am. You create your own hypertension. He got so overtense it made him impotent."

"I'll kill you!"

"That's the least of my worries. I won't say anymore about it and you don't have to talk about it, either. I just said it to try to break through your shell. The hospital isn't doing it, but that's your fault. You won't let it, you won't go half-way to meet it."

"It's not something to worry about," Norris said. "It happens to many men at different times in their life, then when you figure out what your worries are, and work them out, it goes away."

"You, I suppose," Mr Mulwin said, "are the neighborhood champion cocksman. Women see you coming and just lie down and spread their legs."

"Oh Mr Mulwin, I'm sorry about whatever's the matter," Mrs Brice said, "but I sincerely do not care for smut."

Bertha laughed. "You should have been at my college. Would your face be red." She stopped laughing and looked at Mr Mulwin. "I wish you'd fuck off and button up, you old grouch. So there."

"All this filthy talk," Lottie said, "is very tiresome. I can contribute my own problem in the briefest possible span: I want a drink."

"Is drinking a symptom," Mr Brice asked, "or is it more of an illness in itself.?"

"It's both," Lottie said. "No, it isn't. It's a habit that grows on you, and I must say it's a very pleasant habit. Barring, that is, the small embarrassments, such as burning dinner, falling down and not being able to talk straight. But as Bertha might say, what the hell."

"Leave me out of it," Bertha said. "I'm no boozer. Give me good old grass every time. And I wouldn't mind dropping a little acid. You people don't even know what the world *looks* like. Though I admit that last trip when they brought me here was pretty freaky. It scared me shitless. I think it was bum acid. That rat, I should have known better than to buy it off him. If they legalized acid, then you'd know what you were getting, instead of this home brewed stuff. That can kill you. The last choo choo train."

3

The motel room was paneled in knotty pine and decorated with bronzed plaques of Roman emperors. Mag and Norris were lying side by side, she in her slip and he with a towel over his middle. They were both smoking, he his pipe and she a cigarette in a tortoise shell holder. Mag broke what had been a long and easy silence.

"I don't know quite how it is, but you bring out something in me that Bartram never did. We were quite conservative in our lovemak-

ing, though I always enjoyed it. Well, 'always' is saying a lot: there
are times when one partner is in the mood and the other isn't. Don't
you find it so?"

"Comparisons are invidious. And, as I told you, I'm not a person
of wide experience."

"You don't have any regrets, do you? I don't. Not yet, anyway."

"No regrets. And let's see that there aren't any in the future,
either. That's important to me, Mag."

"Sometimes I can't help thinking of you and Lottie, together, I
mean, like this."

"Try not to. My marriage is a contented one, just as yours and
Bartram's was, and it's going to go on being one. You must remember
that, or we'll have to break off now. You're a loving, satisfying,
affectionate woman, Mag, but I'm serious about that."

"Please don't talk as though I were a threat to you. And Lottie. I'm
not. You know people sometime think I'm a silly-billy because I
babble on so, but I can keep my own counsel. You'd be surprised."

"If there's one thing I don't want, it's to be surprised. I hate
surprises and I always have. So if you have any little secrets, please
keep them."

"I do, I do. As I say, you'd be surprised, but I'm not going to
surprise you. That's a promise. Which I'll keep. I saw Maureen
Delahantey uptown today. The shopping that woman has to do to
feed that brood! Did you ever see such a collection of—I won't say
monsters, but, plain big people? Anyway, she got to talking about
our pleasant evening of bridge, and wondered if we shouldn't have
another. She referred to you as the 'grass widower.' She seemed to
think another go would be a good idea, and hinted rather broadly
that it should be at my house this time. Would you be game?"

"Game for a game?"

"Oh Norris, I love your dry wit. Yes, game for another game. *Chez
moi*."

"I don't see why not. Lottie encourages me to go out—she doesn't
expect me to become an eremite, or a troglodyte."

"What's that?"

"A hermit."

"You do seem content to spend quite a few evenings at home alone."

"Truthfully, I'd like to spend more of them with you, Mag, but you know and I know that that isn't possible. This suburb is really quite a small town."

"I'm grateful for small favors. And large. Shall I go ahead and plan a bridge evening? I'll make it dinner, too. I haven't given a dinner party in ever so long."

"I see no objection to it. In fact, I'm all for it. So plan away, little planner."

"Something I never thought I'd be: a woman with a secret life. It's going to be hard going back to being plain Mag Carpenter, widowed home maker who cooks little dinners for one and gets to bed at a decent hour. If this is indecent, I much prefer it."

"Wicked girl."

"I suppose I am, but I don't feel wicked." She ran her hand over his chest. "That's what I like to feel. Some of your chest hairs are gray. I'm going to pull this one out."

"Ouch. They should be gray, at my age. Snow white, in fact."

"Oh, you're not all that old."

"Old enough." Norris pulled the strap of her slip. "What's this?"

"That? That's my breast." Norris nuzzled it, and then replaced the strap.

"Are you planning to sleep in that?"

"This slip? Certainly not. I'm planning to sleep naked, next to you, with just a sheet over us. Sleeping seems such a waste of time, but I'm looking forward to it."

"A good thing. Get that garment off, because I'm about ready to turn off the light. We both have long drives ahead of us in the morning."

"All right my darling lover, Mr Taylor sir."

Chapter V

1

"How do you feel?" Mrs Brice asked. "I think you look more composed today."

"Somewhat better," Lottie said. "Or rather, different. Terribly nervous and as though I might suddenly go on a crying jag. Which isn't like me."

"I was never much for tears, either. Even when the accident happened, and I finally took it in, I stayed dry-eyed. I felt all dried up on the inside. Mr Brice couldn't hold back: how that man wept."

"It might have been better if you had wept, too. Instead of controlling yourself."

"Oh, it wasn't anything I did on purpose. That was how it took me, that was all."

"Coo-ee," said a voice from the sun room door. There stood Maureen and Biddy. "Are we a surprise?" Maureen asked. "A welcome surprise, I mean?"

"Of course, of course. How sweet, how kind. Now don't scoot off,

Mrs Brice. I want you to meet my friends." Lottie made the introductions. "If I seem a little jumpy you musn't mind: I *am* jumpy. Have you a cigarette, Maureen?"

Maureen produced a pack from her purse.

"Mentholated," Lottie said. "Well, any port in a storm. And when I think what I went through giving up cigarettes. But I simply must have someting to do with my hands, before I wring them off."

"Are you neighbors of Mrs Taylor?" Mrs Brice asked.

"Close neighbors and old friends," Biddy said. "How does that saying go? 'Better near neighbors than far friends.' I've never quite understood that."

"It sounds a little too much like 'Anything is better than nothing' to me," said Maureen.

"Near neighbors sometimes become fast friends," Biddy opined.

"Sometimes they remain total strangers," Mrs Brice said. "We never visit with the folks who share our drive. Once Mr Brice went over to tell them their chimney was on fire. I think that's practically the only time we've ever spoken to them. Funny."

"There's probably something about them that makes you want not to become involved," Biddy said. "Some neighbors take advantage and impose."

"Well," Mrs Brice said, "they do go to a different church. And they sometimes give rather loud parties. Once they had a weenie roast in their back yard and had a keg of beer. That's not Mr Brice's or my way."

Lottie, who was smoking her cigarette in a rather feverish way, choked and gasped. "Oh Mrs Judson," she called, "won't you come and join us? Come and meet my friends."

Mrs Judson brought over her chair, which had a plastic seat, and joined the circle. After more introductions she said, "You ladies seem to have so much to say. I haven't. Please pretend I'm not here."

"What attractive beads," Maureen said to her.

"They were my mother's," Mrs Judson said. "They're real amber."

"So I see," Maureen said.

"I've always been partial to amber," Biddy said, "though I never had any of my own. My grandmother's set went to one of my aunts. You can rub it with wool and make sparks. At least, I think so."

Mrs Judson looked alarmed. "Oh, I don't think so. At least, I've never gotten any shocks from it."

"Sparks," Biddy said, "not shocks."

"Oh dear," Mrs Judson said.

"May I have another cigarette, Maureen?" Lottie asked.

"My dear, you are smoking up a storm. Why don't you keep the pack? I have a carton at home."

"If you're sure . . . there's a cart that comes around later and I can buy some. If I can't drink, I suppose I might as well go up in smoke. Excuse me. I'm afraid this transition period is making me rather tiresome.

Bertha passed by. She was wearing a dress for a change, instead of a wrapper. "Hen party," she said, continuing on her way to the phonograph.

"That was Bertha," Mrs Brice said. "She's one of those problem young people you read about in the paper. I must say, I think she's beginning to make real progress." She lowered her voice. "She used to have these kind of fits, and would lie on the floor in the corridor, dead to the world, to all appearances. I found it quite alarming and pitiable, but the doctors seemed to think it was just some sort of attention getting device."

"There's no harm in Bertha," Lottie said, "though one of these evenings I'd like to wash her mouth out with soap."

Mrs Brice giggled. "I'll hold her while you do it."

"There's nothing worse than a vile mouth," Biddy said. "Do you remember the time Bryan did just that to Patrick? Or maybe it was Michael. And I believe all the boy said was, excuse me, damnation."

"I think it was more the tone and spirit in which it was said that angered Bryan," Maureen said. "He's never been one to use much strong language himself; at least, not in front of the boys. He's a little hard on them at times, but he sets a good example."

"Firmness," Biddy said, "my father was a great believer in firmness."

"So was mine," Lottie said. "I wonder if that isn't why I'm here.

(69)

My parents have been gone a long time, but sometimes I still feel an urge to rebel against them. Especially my father. Imagine, a grown woman of my age, and yet sometimes I think of something he said or did, or wouldn't let me do, and I quail. The more I think about him the less I like him, which seems silly, when he's dead. I'm almost glad that Norris and I never had any children, to rear and have grow up and resent you."

"That's just your nerves talking," Biddy said. "I'm sure you were a very devoted daughter. I can always tell. My father was strict, and I'm grateful to him for it. I grew up knowing right from wrong and with certain ingrained habits: regularity, for instance."

Maureen laughed. "Biddy certainly is regular, she never deviates an iota from her schedule. We don't need a clock with Biddy in the house, always the first one down to put the kettle on."

"Oh the Delahanteys and their tea," Lottie said, "they're famous for it."

"I'm like that," Mrs Brice said. "I wouldn't know any peace of mind if my chores weren't done on time. I didn't make a plan when I married and took up housekeeping—the habits just grew. You know what I mean, every Monday morning at ten I find myself sorting out the laundry." She sighed. "Only, with just Mr Brice and myself, the chores don't take up enough time. Some afternoons are very empty."

Maureen and Biddy looked sympathetic, but asked no question. Mr Mulwin came over to the coffee urn, near which they were seated.

"Oh Mr Mulwin, let me introduce you to my friends," Lottie said.

"Haven't got the time," Mr Mulwin said, taking a paper cup and filling it with coffee. "Got to call my office and see who's sneaking off to lunch early." He headed for the pay phone in the hall.

"He's the terror of the ward," Lottie said. "Sooner snap your head off than look at you. But I'm determined to break down his defenses. Underneath all that bearishness, there's an ordinary human being."

"I admire the way you're not afraid to tackle him," Mrs Brice said. "He scares me half to death, just the way he looks at you."

"He's mean," Mrs Judson said. "I don't like mean men."

"I get the impression from Mrs Mulwin," Mrs Brice said, "that he was always a pretty stern proposition. One of those men who has to have everything just so and complains a lot if it isn't. One can see that Mr Taylor, if I may say it, is the soul of consideration."

Lottie laughed. "Oh, Norris has his little quirks, but by and large we rub along together pretty well. He likes his meals on time, that's for certain. Norris tends to expect the worst, and since that rarely happens, he doesn't get upset too easily." Lottie paused. "My husband is a very forbearing man," she said in a different tone of voice.

"You never know what he's thinking," Maureen said, "unlike my Bryan. With him to think is to speak. In fact he doesn't always stop to think."

"It's better that way," Biddy said. "You always know where you stand with Bryan. He's not one of those hush-hush men who keep you guessing. I'm not referring to Norris, Lottie, I have my own husband in mind. It didn't happen often, but ever and again I'd just know something bothered him, and often it would be days before I got to the bottom of it. Something simple, like his collars weren't starched the way he liked them. I used to say to him, 'Just say it, whatever it is. Don't go around making me feel I've committed some crime, when it's only your old collars.' That's how I used to talk to him, dear soul."

"Mr Judson and I suit each other very well," Mrs Judson said, and blushed.

"Lottie," Maureen said, "I'm beginning to think this is more of a club than a hospital—interesting new friends, such a relaxed atmosphere . . ."

Mr Mulwin came roaring into the room. "You wouldn't believe," he more or less yelled at Lottie, "if I told you what's going on in that office." He then charged down the room and ordered Bertha either to turn down the phonograph or turn it off.

Bertha continued weaving back and forth. "You don't own this room," she said. "I have my rights here just as much as you, and one of them is dancing."

Mr Mulwin reached out and turned the phonograph way down. Bertha turned it up as loud as it would go, and began to scream. "Werewolf!" was one of the words that emerged. As though from

(71)

nowhere, a hefty nurse appeared, just as Mr Mulwin was retorting with "Foul mouthed bitch."

"Turn that thing down," the nurse said. "I want you each to go to your rooms until you've collected yourselves." Mr Mulwin had left before the nurse finished speaking, muttering about his blood pressure.

"You can't make me," Bertha said. "Anyway, he yelled at me first."

"I don't want to force you," the nurse said, "I'm asking you."

"When I want to go to my room and lie down you won't let me. When I want to play the phonograph and dance, you make me go to my room. That's supposed to make sense?"

"It will shortly be lunch time, and I want you to be able to eat a nice quiet meal. You know you feel better when you co-operate in these little matters, Bertha." Looking sullen, Bertha left the room.

"I'm afraid you've seen us not at our best," the nurse said to Lottie's little group. "But we have these little gusts now and then. Visiting time will be up shortly." She smiled and left.

Lottie, who had lit another cigarette, said, "What were you saying Maureen, about the relaxed atmosphere? You should have been here trying to sleep the night Bertha had her screaming fits. They had to put her in one of the locked rooms."

"Locked rooms!" Mrs Judson said.

"You don't have to worry about those," Mrs Brice said. "It's just for some of the hyper-active patients, who might hurt themselves—or someone else."

"Oh dear," Mrs Judson said.

"That was exciting," Biddy said. "Somehow that's more the way I thought things would be."

"Raving lunatics?" Lottie said. "We can supply on demand."

Maureen gathered herself together. "Time for us to run. Can I bring you anything? Do you have enough to read?"

"Not a thing," Lottie said. "We're awash in magazines and paperbacks. Anyway, I can't fix my attention for more than ten minutes at a time."

"You're looking wonderfully well, and I'm sure these feelings of—of jumpiness will pass off quite soon. I'm tempted to check in here for a rest myself. The twins have been more than usually impossible. It's like being a referee at a wrestling match. Come along, Biddy, we don't want that nurse chasing us out."

Biddy hopped to her feet. "And she certainly looks like she could do it. Very pleased to meet you, Mrs Brice, Mrs Judson. We'll be looking in again."

2

The Delehanteys had reached the dessert course: tapioca cream. Bryan spooned his up with avidity, at the same time enjoining the twins to go slow. "And how was our neighbor, the patient?"

"Lottie's put on weight," Maureen said. "I imagine hospital food is quite starchy. I suppose she'll be able to get it off when she comes home and gets onto a regular diet. Physically, she seemed in fine shape, but so nervous, so jumpy. My heart went out to her. It makes one wonder about drinking, if those are the risks involved."

"Is Mrs Taylor away because of drinking?" Patrick asked.

"That's no problem of yours," Bryan said. "And stop sucking that out of the side of your spoon. Put the spoon in your mouth, then take it out. Slobberer."

"It's no secret," Maureen said. "For some people alcohol can become an illness—it poisons their system. Then they need treatment to recover."

"We learned about it in biology," Michael said. "Maybe she'll have to join Alcoholics Anonymous. There's one in town. They meet on Wednesday evening in the basement of the Methodist church. I wonder what they talk about? The good old days?"

Bryan laughed. "Don't make jokes," he said, "about Mrs Taylor. She's a sick woman and a good friend."

"In many ways," Biddy said, "it was a most interesting visit. All types and conditions of men. And women. Some you might meet in your own parlor and not think a thing about it. Others—there was this man who, as the boys say, completely blew his stack."

"He was a Mr Mulwin," Maureen interposed.

"Yes," Biddy said, "that was the name. A Mrs Judson, a lady with whom we became acquainted, was quite alarmed by his ranting. But I could tell it was all just a show. I've seen men like that before. The loud kind. All you have to do is stand up to them and they back down quick enough. I was sorriest for Mrs. Judson—painfully shy with a lovely string of old-fashioned amber beads. Then there was another quiet lady, a Mrs Brice, but she had more to say for herself. Seemed like a widow to me."

"No," Maureen said, "I don't think so. I'm sure she mentioned a Mr Brice. Whom I took to be her husband. Or perhaps it was the way she said 'we' about something. But I'm certain she's not a widow."

"Had any calls from the merry widow?" Bryan asked.

"Mag? As a matter of fact, I did. We had a nice chat. She seems even cheerier than ever and wants to get up another bridge evening, at her house. She seems quite concerned about Norris, and how lonely his evenings must be."

"He's always got that dog for company," Bryan said. "God, it's disgusting how fat they let her get. More like a pig than a dog."

"Bassets are like that," his mother said. "After a certain age, they sag."

"I wouldn't want a basset," Patrick said. "I'd rather have a German shepherd."

"Which you would be the one to take care of, I suppose," Bryan said.

"Sure. Can we get one?"

"No. One pet is enough. Anyway, Twing would tear it to ribbons."

"The Tromper kids each have their own pet," Patrick persisted. "There are five of them—three dogs and two cats. They get along all right."

"I've been in the Trompers' house," Maureen said, "and the answer is no, no a thousand times no. One thing you have to say about Twingy-poo is that she's neat and clean as a pin."

"Twing got in our room last night," Michael said. "She slept on my bed and kept me awake. She kept playing with my toes through

(74)

the blanket and digging her claws in."

"Why didn't you put her in the kitchen, Mr Lazy?" Bryan said.

"I was too sleepy. She didn't wake me up that much."

"Oh dear," Maureen said. "I know Twing doesn't have fleas, but I don't like the idea that she might have, and have them got into the bed clothes. The catch on the kitchen door has to be fixed."

"I'll look at it," Bryan said.

"I hope you'll do more than look at it."

"I can't do much about it until I have looked at it. If you close it firmly, it catches."

"I put Twing in the kitchen myself last night," Biddy said. "And I closed the door and gave it a shake to test it. The latch just pops open of itself. I think you may have to rehang the whole door."

"That will be fun," Bryan said, "a wonderful way to spend my day off. Why don't you call up Mr What's-his-name the carpenter and have him look at it? He can probably fix it in a jiffy."

"You're the one who said you'd look at it. If I call the carpenter he says he'll come and then he never shows up. They're all like that."

"In my day," Biddy said, "there was always a handyman in town you could send for when anything went wrong. Mr Moxter was the one we used. A grim silent man, but he could mend anything— plumbing, the electric, hardware. I remember when he installed a new lock on the front door and come evening he wasn't finished. 'Don't tell me,' I said, 'I'm going to have to spend a night alone with my babies in an unlocked house?' Bryan's father was off somewhere on a business trip. All he said was, 'If anybody's determined to get in, they'll find a way,' and off he went with his tools. I pushed the upright piano up against the door. All the same, I didn't get a wink of sleep. And the funny thing is, I never felt a bit frightened alone in the house when my husband was called away on business. Except that one time. The next day Mr Moxter finished the job. 'Feel any safer?' he said. 'I certainly do,' I said, 'and if I'd known it was an all day job, I would have had you come in the morning instead of starting it after lunch.' I said it right to his face, I was that peeved."

"Biddy," Maureen said, "you're a fund of memories, it's a marvel to me. Don't ask me what I did last week: I haven't a clue."

"You played bridge with Mag and Norris," Bryan said. "And we went to see that awful movie you'd been hankering about."

"I loved it," Maureen said. "A nice weepy. Though I think they should have told her right out, when they knew she had cancer."

"Where are you going?" Bryan said to Patrick.

"To put the kettle on."

"It's already on," Maureen said. "As long as you're up, you can make the tea."

"And don't put all the tea there is in the pot," Bryan said, "I don't like tea you can float an egg on."

"You don't like it weak, either," Biddy said. "None of us do."

"I had coffee for breakfast when I slept over at Nick Tromper's," Michael said. "I didn't like to ask for tea, special. Though I guess Mrs Tromper would have made it if I had. Asked for it."

"No, that was the right thing. Always eat what your host offers you. Did you drink it black?"

Michael made a face. "No. I put in plenty of cream and sugar. It wasn't bad. I liked it, I think."

Twing leapt into the center of the table. "No," Bryan said, "not on the table, kitty. Come sit in my lap." The cat curled up there and allowed itself to be scratched behind the ear.

The evening sun came in through the sheer glass curtains and sparkled on the silver, the dishes and the glassware.

"Why look," Biddy said, "there's a rainbow in the water pitcher," which was of Norsk crystal. "Isn't that the loveliest thing!"

3

Group was in session, and Dr Kearney looked bored. "All right, Bertha," he said, "you've made yourself the center of attention long enough. We've all heard your stories of marijuana, music and LSD. You've convinced us that you were a real swinger, and you swung yourself right in here."

"You never talk about your problems, I've noticed," Lottie said, "the things behind your actions. That might be more interesting—

(76)

and helpful. To all of us, not just yourself."

"My only problem," Bertha said, "is that I have a family. They're nice, but they bug me."

"Bug you?" Mrs Brice said.

"They let me do anything I want, but all the time I can tell they secretly disapprove. They don't know what to make of *me*, but I know what to make of *them*. Spineless. Nice, but spineless."

"We haven't heard much from you, Mrs Judson," Dr Kearney said.

"I never did talk much," Mrs Judson said.

"That's true," Sam Judson said. "Ethel was never much of a talker. She shows her feelings in other ways."

"In other ways?" Norris said. "I'd be interested to hear an example."

"In lots—in all kinds of little ways. Like making something special for dinner I like we haven't had lately. Or baking a cake for a neighbor. Ethel's a great baker. And she never raised her voice to the children, but they never sassed her or took advantage."

"You have children?" Lottie said.

"Three," Sam said. "Grown up, married and moved away."

"They keep in touch," Mrs Judson said. "Very thoughtful, all of them. My living room is a bower on Mother's Day. Easter, too."

"Your life seems empty to you," Lottie said, "without them. It's a shame none of them live in the town. Norris and I wanted to have children, very much at one time, but it didn't happen. I've thought that if I had had children, then my days wouldn't have been so empty—just me and the house and Norris away at the office. I started nipping at the bottle, to perk myself up in the afternoon. Business men have martinis at lunch, I used to tell myself, where's the harm? But now I see if we had children, they'd be grown up now and gone and I'd be the same old person I am, Mary Charlotte Taylor, lady drunk."

"You sure feel sorry for yourself," Bertha said. "All you have to do is kick the habit and you've got it made."

"Yes," Lottie said in what was for her a chastened voice, "that is all I have to do. Somehow it isn't easy, though I have a happy, fortunate

(77)

life."

"You'll be making a new life," Mrs Brice said. "You'll see. You're a warm person, you'll find interests."

"I'm tempted to say," Lottie said, "like what?"

"Perhaps some kind of social work," Mrs Brice said.

"I don't think I'd care for going around poking my nose in other people's business. I'm not the type."

"Things will fall into place," Mrs Brice said, "when you're back at your own home with your own things."

"My things, good grief. There are enough of them. The truth is all I think about is how much I want a drink."

"That's part of this phase," Norris said. "It will pass."

"I wonder," Lottie said.

"That," Dr Kearney said, "largely depends on you, doesn't it? You know as a rule we don't treat alcoholic patients here—you're by way of an experiment."

"Don't count on me not to let down the team," Lottie said. "Right now I'm not making any promises. Mr Mulwin, all evening you've been sitting there glowering and sneering at me. Why you do it doesn't interest me, but I would like to say that, in my opinion, you are an almost perfect bastard."

"Why Lottie," Norris said.

"Please don't provoke my husband," Mrs Mulwin said. "His problems are every bit as real as yours."

"Realer," Mr Mulwin said. "But that's my business."

"Oh dear," Mrs Judson said. "You see, Sam? I told you what it's like. Even the nice ones come out with these awful things."

"I don't call a little snappy exchange," Sam Judson said, "anything so awful. You ought to hear me and Walt—my head salesman— when we get p.o.'d with each other. The fur may not fly but the language gets pretty hot."

"You never talk—you know—dirty around me, Sam," his wife said.

"Certainly not. Business is one thing and home is another. Business is a man's world."

"Male chauvinist pig—typical," Bertha remarked casually.

"*My* business is a man's world," Sam said. "At least I've never met or even heard of a lady car dealer."

"We could be just as good at it as any man," Bertha said. "Probably better. Women are very good salesmen—that's because they're always on the make. If women can sell pantyhose, why not cars?"

"That's what I might do," Lottie said, "when I'm all cured and free—open a used car lot. But I suppose you're expected to stand the customers a drink, so that let's that out. Maybe I'll open a jellies and garden produce stand in front of the lot by the hedge—that would wake the neighborhood up."

"I hate to dash cold water on your scheme," Norris said, "but you'll find we're zoned against commercial enterprises."

"So much for that. I'll have to look further afield. I could become a picket and carry a placard."

"Do you really think," Dr Kearney said, "that flippancy is going to help you get well? It seems to me you're wasting our time as well as your own."

"I get the message," Lottie said. "First you tell Bertha to shut up, now you tell me. All right, see what you can get out of the Mulwin or Mrs Judson."

"Why Mrs Taylor," Mrs Judson said, "how unkind."

"That wasn't like you," Mrs Brice said.

"I've had my say for the evening," Lottie said. "I'll apologize some other time, should I get to feeling like it. No, I do feel like it. I'm sorry if I sounded rude, Mrs Judson. It's my nerves."

"What about me?" Mr Mulwin said.

"My lips are sealed," Lottie said.

"That's a welcome change," Mr Mulwin said. "I for one am heartily sick of your yak-yakety-yak. At least you've climbed down from your lady bountiful pedestal, the one whose helpfulness is going to cure everybody with a nice game of bridge."

"Do you play bridge?" Norris said.

"Maybe I do and maybe I don't."

"He prefers pinochle," Mrs Mulwin said.

"At last we know something about the redoubtable Mr Mulwin," Norris said.

"Sam and I and a few friends enjoy a nice game of pinochle now and then," Mrs Judson said. "It makes an evening pass pleasantly."

"That was one of the things Ethel kind of lost interest in before she came here," Sam said. "All her little interests didn't interest her anymore. When we'd get an invitation she'd excuse herself. It got so she didn't do anything else but brood."

"Withdrawn," Bertha said. "I was never that. Natively, I'm an outgoing person. So is Mr Mulwin, if he'd let himself."

"I haven't got any problems that are going to get licked here. I think I have an ulcer. I feel like there's a cannon ball right in my middle, here."

"Greg, it's your old tension pains," Mrs Mulwin said. "You know what the family doctor said about them—you take things too hard. When you're back home we might take up bowling. That's good exercise."

"For your peace of mind," Dr Kearney said, "I can tell you that you do not have an ulcer."

"What kind of peace of mind is that supposed to give?" Mr Mulwin said. "I have all the pain and symptoms of one, I might as well have the ulcer."

"That's silly talk," Mrs Mulwin said. "You're here to clear up the tensions, not talk about imaginary illnesses."

Mrs Judson's eyes had become watery. "I thought we were friends," she said to Lottie.

"We are," Lottie said.

"But you picked on me."

"You'll have to bear with me—I'm not altogether myself a lot of the time lately. At three in the afternoon my mind goes booze, booze, booze. I can taste it, and it tastes good."

"I'll get wifey here to slip you a bottle," Mr Mulwin said.

"You do, and I'll crack it over your skull," Norris said.

Mr Mulwin laughed. "You two," he said, "are a sketch. Mr and Mrs Uptight Taylor."

"Why did you come here, Mr Mulwin?" Mrs Brice asked. "Don't you want help, don't you want to get well? I didn't even know I was sick when I came here—I knew I was in the dumps, but I thought it was just the blues."

"The blues," Dr Kearney said, "is a good term for it. And when you have them all the time, you want to get rid of them: right?"

"No," Mrs Brice said. "It was Mr Brice's idea that I come here. He could see I was worse off than I knew."

"Yes, Mother," Mr Brice said, "you weren't at all yourself. All our married life you always had a bright word, then, after the accident . . ."

"The accident. I won't ever get over that. But I begin to see that mooning over it won't bring them back. They're gone. Forever. Thad and all his lovely family. The babies. It just seemed so wrong to me, a useless old woman, and they were the ones who were taken. I don't know what people mean by God's infinite mercy. I'm not going to think about it. I'll keep going to church, but I won't think about that."

"I don't believe in God," Bertha said. "Do you, Mr Mulwin?"

"Sure," Mr Mulwin said. "Why not? We're not church goers though. I like to get my sleep Sunday morning."

"Why Greg," Mrs Mulwin said, "we never miss Easter. Or Christmas, usually. And of course we go to a lot of church suppers, and sociables, and like that. Mostly Methodist, but we're not strict about it."

"Everyone's entitled to their opinions," Mrs Brice said.

"It's my opinion," Mr Mulwin said, "that going to church isn't worth much. I don't like being preached at. Too much like school."

"It gives me," Mr Brice said, "a feeling of peace and a deep sense of the mystery of things."

"I'm not a church-goer," Norris said, "But thinking about God gives me similar feelings."

"I didn't know you ever thought about God, Norris," Lottie said.

"Work is prayer," Mrs Brice said. "Good works, that is. I was taught that in Sunday school, and never forgot it. So someone who is doing the right thing, might in a sense be praying, and believing in God, without even knowing it."

"My work is rather mundane for that," Norris said. "I wonder if selling used cars comes under the heading of work is prayer?"

(81)

"As much as anything you do," Gregory Mulwin said. "What is it you do, anyway, unless it's some sort of dark secret."

"I was teasing Sam Judson," Norris said. "Not speaking to you."

"Norris is a lawyer—an attorney," Lottie said, not without pride.

"Largely concerned with real estate," Norris added.

"A shyster," Mr Mulwin said. "I've come up against a few of your kind in my day and thanks, but no thanks."

"If you were to buy a home, or to sell the building in which you have your business, you might find a reputable lawyer quite a useful person to know. There's much written between the lines of that fine print."

"People often sign things," Lottie said, "without the slightest idea of what they're letting themselves in for. Norris has told me of some hair raising instances."

"I don't believe in private property," Bertha said. "Everything ought to belong to everybody, like a commune."

"I don't hold with communism," Mrs Brice said, "but it does seem wrong that some people work very hard all their lives and have nothing to show for it. That's never seemed quite right to me."

"And the last shall be first," Mr Brice murmured.

"And the rest of us will bring up the rear, lugging our TV sets," Norris said.

"I've never cared all that much about TV," Lottie said. "Though doubtless I have as many spiritual faults as the next. The next world: I can't say I spend all that much time thinking about it."

"I do," Mrs Brice said. "Though I couldn't express my thoughts in words."

"Some thoughts don't need to be, Mother," Mr Brice said.

"Do you think we could return to the more immediate problems of this world?" Dr Kearney said. "This is a hospital, not a seminary."

"Oh dear," Mrs Judson said, "and just when I was getting interested."

"You're more interested in the spiritual life than in this one?" Dr Kearney said. "Or to put it another way, you make a choice between them?"

"I'm not sure I know what you mean."

"He means," Sam Judson said, "aren't your problems ones of this world, the one with automobiles and houses in it, rather than of some other world, one we don't know much about?"

"Oh dear," Mrs Judson said. "I miss my quiet living room and my chair, even if I did feel sad, sitting there."

"Can you tell us what you felt sad about?" Norris asked. "You and Mr Judson seem an affectionate couple."

"Of course we are," Mrs Judson said. "Don't put words in my mouth—I never said Mr Judson made me sad. It was just—it was only—well, it wasn't any one thing. My life is more than half over, at best, and the half that's over *was* the *best* half. Having babies and a family all around you to take care of. The there was less and less to do, and I got the mopes. Or the blues, if you want to call it that, Dr Kearney. I didn't plan it to happen: it crept up on me gradually, like mud. I'm sorry now I said I wanted to kill myself, but I was feeling agitated that day and it popped out without my thinking. I wouldn't know how to do it. Besides, I wouldn't do it anyway. It would make Mr Judson unhappy."

"Very unhappy, dear."

"I think a person ought to have the right to go when they want to go," Mr Mulwin said. "I think that's a basic human right. I don't want to go myself, just yet, but if I did want to go, I'd go."

"Oh Greg," his wife said, "suicide is the act of someone in a disturbed state of mind. Nobody who was feeling himself would want to do that: you never know what tomorrow holds."

"Oh yes you do," Lottie said. "That's the trouble."

"I may be sick as a dog, but I'm as happy as a king," Bertha said. She began to whistle a rock tune.

"It seems to me," Mrs Brice said, "that the thing is to find an interest that takes you out of yourself. I was thinking I might become one of the ladies who help out part time in the hospital, like that nice woman who comes around with the book cart. What are they called, candy stripers?"

"Candy stripers?" Norris said.

"They wear an attractive red and white striped kind of smock," Mrs Brice explained, "striped like spearmint candy."

(83)

"I'm not so advanced as you," Lottie said. "At the moment all activities strike me as repulsive."

"I just don't know," Mrs Judson said. "I've never been a good mixer."

"My outside activities," Mr Mulwin said, "are ruining my business, and the sooner I get back to it, the better."

"Wasn't it partly anxiety about your business," Dr Kearney asked, "that got you in here."

"Yes, it was," Mrs Mulwin said. "Mr Mulwin finds it hard to rely on others—he double-checks and feels he has to carry the whole show on his own two shoulders."

"You talk like I never tried to relax. I have tried. Some people aren't cut out for relaxation, they like to keep on the move, to keep busy. I'm one of that kind. Only I get the lump."

"The lump?" Mrs Brice said.

"Right here," he placed a hand on his solar plexus. "Then I get short tempered and angry. You can't get the best out of people who work for you if you're snitified all the time, I know that. But I get the lump and it seems like I have to take it out on whoever's next to me. It's not my fault."

"Of course not, dear," Mrs Mulwin said. "It's not a question of fault."

"You ought to try exercises," Lottie said, "like yoga. *Make* yourself relax."

"Oh Christ," Mr Mulwin said, "will you please stop trying to help me? You're quite a mess yourself."

"And don't I know it," Lottie said. "OK. I'll quit. I still don't think you're as black as you paint yourself."

"I'm a suffering hunk of humanity and if I'm painted any color it's not black, it's gray."

"The trouble with you is," Bertha said to Mr Mulwin, "you think you're something special. Well, I have news for you. You're not. I get a lump too but I don't go bragging about it."

"I don't think my husband was exactly bragging about it, Bertha," Mrs Mulwin said.

"I haven't had one of my spells lately," Bertha said. "That must

(84)

mean I'm better than whatever I was. But I don't feel better. I feel crazy. My voices keep telling me different things and they can't agree. I'd be lost without my voices."

"I hear voices," Mr Mulwin said, "sometimes just when I'm dropping off to sleep. Last night one of them called me a lot of foul names. The funny thing was, until I woke all the way I thought it was the night nurse—that husky male one—who was doing it. Calling me names."

"What do you make of it?" Dr Kearney said.

"I don't think that male nurse likes me. I was crabby with him one night and he kind of snarled at me."

"But it wasn't his voice you heard last night."

"Well, I guess I expected him to say mean things to me, after that time, and kind of dreamed that he did. I couldn't repeat to you the things he said. I mean, the voices. The voice. There was just one."

"Sometimes," Mrs Brice said, "when I'm dropping off I hear a voice. It says my name. It startles me. Then I get back to going to sleep."

"It's probably the beginning of the dream process," Lottie said. "I have fascinating dreams—nightmares, happy dreams, dreams that are like the movies—but in the morning I can't remember them. It's frustrating."

"Once in a great while," Norris said, "Lottie talks in her sleep. Usually it makes very little sense, although once in the canning season she said quite loudly, 'It will never jell.' "

"It never did, either," Lottie said. "It was quince."

"Yetch," Bertha said. "I hate quince jelly. I don't see how anybody can stand to eat it."

There was a pause, in which Lottie was heard humming to herself. It was the old song, "I had a little drink about an hour ago . . ."

"You have got a one-track mind," Mr Mulwin said.

"I've never pretended otherwise. Look, I wish you'd make an effort to be a little friendly toward me. I don't like going around all the time, feeling that someone is giving off bad vibrations, directed at me."

"I just say what I think," Mr Mulwin said. "That's the way I'm built."

"Yes, that's true," Mrs Mulwin said. "You musn't mind: some things he says to me roll off me like water off a duck's back."

"Anyway," Mr Mulwin went on, "you start it: always trying to be so damned helpful. 'Oh Mr Mulwin, come learn to play bridge, it'll do you good.' I haven't got time to learn to play bridge, even if I wanted to. And I don't like fuss budget do-gooders. Why don't you work on Bertha and Mrs Judson and leave me alone?"

"None of the patients is obliged to talk to the others," Dr Kearney said, "but it seems a healthy sign to me when they do. Hostility and chronic anger are symptoms."

"Symptoms of what?" Mr Mulwin demanded.

"Of a nature not at home with itself, I'd say," Dr Kearney replied.

"Can't I join one of the other groups?" Mrs Judson asked in a quavering voice. "Maybe I'd make more progress. There's so much acrimony here."

"We can discuss that in our private session," Dr Kearney said. "It's not altogether out of the question. Though I think you'd find the other groups are also composed of more or less troubled human beings."

"I don't feel like a human being," Mrs Judson said.

"What do you feel like?" Mr Brice asked.

"A dead animal. Well, not quite dead. I wish I could hibernate, like a bear."

"Summer would come," Norris said. "It always does. No animal both hibernates and estivates."

"I'd like to," Lottie said. "Oh, I don't mean that, Norris. I want to feel the way I used to, only perhaps I'm too old. I'm tired of feeling tormented, or tormenting myself, or whatever it is that's going on. I know people get cured of their craving for alcohol, but I don't believe it, not for myself, not on the inside."

"It will wear away gradually," Norris said. "When you're out of here you'll be free to drink or not, as you please, and when you find you can do without it, I expect you'll feel an enormous sense of accomplishment."

"But suppose I don't?" Lottie said. "I mean, suppose I do take a drink—go on a quiet lady-like bat? I'd like to go on a toot, right now."

"If you fall down," Norris said, "you can get up again. But I don't think you will. I know you better than that."

"Why not try yoga, Mrs Taylor?" Mr Mulwin said.

"I may. I'm quite limber for a person my age."

"That's out for me," Mrs Brice said. "I could never contort these old bones into those weird positions. Running the vacuum under the sofa makes me wonder if I'm ever going to straigten up again."

"Mr Brice should give you alcohol rubs," Mrs Judson said. "I give them to Sam, and he says they help a lot. Especially after he's been doing yard work."

"Let's play a game," Bertha said. "Everybody tell one wish—something you want, or wish would happen—any kind of wish. I'll start. I wish I was a rock star."

"I wish," Mr Mulwin said, "we could cut the games and get down to business. If these sessions are doing anybody any good, I'm a monkey's uncle."

"You sure are," Bertha said.

"Everybody knows what I wish," Lottie said. "You can make it a whisky sour, straight up. While you're at it, you might as well make it a double."

"I wish I didn't have to be here," Mrs Judson said. "And that people could get along better with each other."

"I can't bring myself to say I wish the accident had never happened," Mrs Brice said, "somehow, it seems irreligious. It would be childish. I guess what I wish is that I could become resigned."

"That's not a very positive wish, Mother," Mr Brice said.

"Maybe not. There isn't anything I want. I couldn't say I wish I was a good bridge player. I wouldn't be sincere. Oh I'll pick that. I wish I was good at cards. How dreary it sounds to me."

"Well, Bertha," Mr Mulwin said, "we played your little game. Feel better?"

"Much. Only you didn't play it fair. I knew you wouldn't make a real wish."

"OK. I wish I could get this cannon ball out of my guts."

"Stop thinking about it," Bertha said, "and it will go away."

"Fat lot you know about it," Mr Mulwin said.

Chapter VI

1

Norris's phone buzzed and his secretary said, "A Mrs Carpenter is on the line."

"Put her through. Mag? What can I do for you?"

"Believe it or not, this is by way of being a business call. I want to make changes in my will. I've never been all that crazy about Bartram's lawyer, he's sort of an old fuddy-duddy who talks down to me, so I thought, 'Why not call on a friend?' You being the friend in question. I know you're ever so successful, but every little bit of business helps, doesn't it?"

"Yes and no. You see, Mag, we rather specialize in realty, and don't do much in the testamentary line."

"Ah! 'Don't do much.' Then you do do some. Couldn't you make an exception for a friend? It would give me such confidence, knowing my affairs are in your hands."

"I'm not a broker, you know."

"Now, now, don't tease. Just say, yes, you'll do me this little favor, and we can make an appointment. I'll have to get my will out of the vault, and it's too late to do it today."

"I see there's no gainsaying you, Mag. When would you like to come by? Say, tomorrow at three?"

"Tomorrow at three. Perhaps we could have lunch first?"

"That, I'm afraid is out. I'm lunching with a business associate."

"As a matter of fact, Norris, I'm quite nearby. I came in to shop and I'm at Lathem's. Can I talk you into coming out for a cup of coffee or a drink?"

"That doesn't sound so wise to me."

"Oh, just this once. I'm not setting any precedent: you needn't fear I'll call you every other day, trying to lure you away from your desk. I know you're busy. But just this once. That can't hurt."

"If you mean it, just this once, then all right. Perhaps we better have a little chat."

"I think I'd prefer a drink to coffee," Mag said. "Why not the Chez Ami? No one will be there this time of the day."

When Norris got to the darkened bar, all red plush and white plaster swags, Mag was the only customer. She was sitting in an intimate booth, toward the back.

After they had ordered (a whisky sour for Norris, a vodka martini on the rocks for Mag), Norris said, "I'm both annnoyed and disappointed with you. To date, we've been moderately discreet, a thing desired by both of us, and essential to me. I call this anything but circumspect, it's obvious, it's risky, it's foolish. I am, really, angry with you. If events are going to take this turn, then we are going to cut everything short, right now."

"Oh Norris, don't talk like that. I'll cry."

"Oh great. That's all I need. To have some acquaintance walk in and find me with a wailing woman in a dark bar in the middle of the afternoon. How long do you think it takes a story like that to get around? I don't want to be talked about myself, I don't want you to be talked about, and what's between us is never going to reach Lottie's ears. Not if I can help it. You'd better remind yourself that you're having a fling with a very much married man."

"Norris, for the love of God, stop. I'll lose control of my emotions.

Norris, I'm in love with you. Have a little pity."

"Couldn't this have kept until our next meeting? I've told you how I feel about you. But if hysteria is going to rear its lovely head, we're through. I mean that, Mag."

"Yes. You make it very plain."

"I know you're impulsive, even flighty, but you've got a lot of control as well. It showed in the way you handled yourself when Bartram passed on. Call on that will-power of yours, and we'll both be happier. We've had some good times together, Mag. Don't mess it up."

"And we're going to have more. Look. I'm chastised. I'm sorry I was impulsive—it seemed innocent enough when it occurred to me to call you. Surely a lawyer sometimes has a drink with a client? At least, that's how it seemed to me. I even said, on the phone, I'm not setting any precedents."

"That," Norris said, "you can say again."

"All right, I will. This is no precedent. Just a quiet drink between friends and neighbors. And I'd like another drink. I'm miserable."

"It seems to me you're drinking more than you used to. You better watch it."

"Is that how you nagged Lottie into the sanatorium?"

"That's the remark of a bitch. I'm going back to my office."

"Oh Norris, I am sorry. I didn't mean that at all. I know it wasn't that way. I felt a sudden flare of anger at your bawling me out and had to say something. I do, do apologize. Sincerely. Please, dear. Stay."

Norris made no reply, but flagged the waiter and ordered two more drinks. "OK Mag. I was rough on you. End of lecture. With the proviso that if I said some hard things, I meant them. Now to pastures new. What were you shopping for?"

"Oh, a dress and some other things I scarcely need. And I returned a defective hair drier. Filling in time. Shopping is practically a full time job for a widow. The girl at the exchange window at Lathem's gave me a 'What, you again?' look. I couldn't have cared less. I see no reason to keep a machine that doesn't work. Why, it might have been dangerous."

"You were right to return it. Oh no. Bryan Delehantey just walked in the door and if you think he doesn't see us think again. He's trying to decide whether to pretend he hasn't seen me. Can't have that." Norris stood up and waved, and Bryan joined them.

"Bryan," Norris said, "I'd like to introduce you to a client of mine: Mrs Carpenter, this is Bryan Delahantey: Bryan, Mag Carpenter."

"Client, eh?" Bryan said. "Hope you're not thinking of selling your house, Mag. I know realty is Norris' big number."

"Heavens no," Mag said. "Not as long as I can still creak up the stairs. I put years of my life into creating my own haven and nothing is going to prise me out of it."

"I think I'll order a drink," Bryan said, and did so: rye and water.

"It was too silly," Mag went on. "But last night, I don't know what made me think of it—I was brushing my hair—it dawned on me that I've never changed my will since Bartram passed on. And of course Bartram was my legatee. That would leave a fine kettle of fish if I was knocked down by a car one of these fine days. I have some cousins who would doubtless get it all if I left that kind of will and, while I plan to remember them, we're not all *that* close. No one could accuse me of being a wealthy woman, but Bartram did leave me comfortably off."

"Yes," Bryan said, "Bartram had a fine head for business. He was much respected, and is much missed."

"Yes," Mag said, "much, much missed."

"Well, Norris," Bryan said, "you're a gay dog, cutting out of the office with a beautiful widow."

"Every dog has his day," Norris said. "And one might ask what brings you here? A hair of the dog that bit you? Were you bitten last night?"

"Haven't had a hangover since I was in college. Not what you could call a real hangover. No, Maureen's in town shopping so we're going to have an early supper and catch a show." At these words, Maureen entered.

"This is a surprise," she said. "You two joining us for a little quiet revelry?"

"Not me," Norris said. "I've still got an hour's work on my desk, then it's one of my evenings at the hospital. Family group therapy. Very instructive. Also, rather bizarre."

"I wouldn't dream of breaking in on your date with your beau, Maureen. I know how rarely you two must get a chance to spend an evening out together. Besides, I'm done in my Lathem's. I just want a supper on a tray and watch a little TV, if I can keep my eyes open."

"Oh, were you at Lathem's too?" Maureen said, sipping the margarita she had ordered.

"I tried on more tacky hats than I would care to count," Mag said. "After a while I began to think it wasn't the hats, it was me. In the end I didn't buy a thing, though there is a suit I may go back and try on again. I'm not sure I need it, but a suit always comes in hands. Navy, piped with white."

"Sounds smart," Maureen said, "just your style."

"Perhaps we could come in together one day, and you could tell me what you really think."

"That might be nice," Maureen said.

"Ladies and gentleman," Norris said, "as the walrus said, the time has come. I can hear my desk calling like a demon lover. Mag, thanks for your company, and I'll expect you tomorrow at three sharp, bearing the documents in the case." Norris put some money on the table, made his farewells, and left.

"If I'm going to beat the traffic," Mag said, "I'd best be on my way. I hate getting caught in a jam."

"Sure you won't change your mind and join us?" Bryan said.

"Yes," Maureen said, "please do. I've forgotten the name of the movie we're going to see, but it's said to be very fine. One of the more serious kind of westerns."

"It's dear of you to insist," Mag said, "but no, I won't, I really won't. Actually this matter of my will has made me rather blue, it brings back memories, and all I want is to crawl into my hidey-hole and hope that it will soon be tomorrow."

"You'll feel better then," Maureen said. "I'm sure of that. You're a resilient person. I always admire you for it, and Biddy often remarks on it."

"Dear Biddy: remember me to her." And with that, Mag too made her farewells.

When Mag had re-entered the sunlit street, Maureen said, "Well!"

"What do you mean, 'Well'?" Bryan asked.

"I mean what do you suppose that was all about? If I know one thing about Mag Carpenter, she changed that will the day after she buried Bartram. Those little feminine ways thinly cloak one of the most practical little women I've ever come up against."

"You're nuts," Bryan said. "I mean, if you're implying there's any carrying on between Mag and Norris. Demon lover indeed. Just the fact that they'd be in a place like this together, at this time of day, proves it. If they had a guilty secret, they'd take more care to keep it hidden. No, I'm not buying."

"It still seems funny to me. Lottie told me about a peculiar visit Mag paid her at the hospital—wasn't herself at all, and more or less fled as soon as she arrived."

"Hospitals make some people nervous. They do me. In fact, I'm glad you haven't asked me to go with you and visit her. Hospitals don't scare me, I just don't like them."

"That's because you're so naturally healthy, Bryan. I can tell you one thing: Mag Carpenter is interested in Norris, and she'd better watch her step. Nobody can pull any wool over Mary Charlotte Taylor's eyes."

2

"It's beyond me," Mrs Judson said.

Lottie put down her paint brush. "It's not beyond you," she said. "I'll lend a hand and start you out."

"Oh," said Miss Pride, who was more or less in charge of creative therapy, "I'm sure Mrs Judson can work it out. Why don't we give her a chance to try it on her own."

"She has," Lottie said. "I don't think a little intra-patient co-operation will do any harm; in fact, I believe it's encouraged around here."

Miss Pride, who was young and easily cowed, went off to help an advanced senility case with the finger paints.

"It's beyond me," Mrs Judson repeated. Before her lay the makings of a moccasin: stamped out pieces of leather, some thongs, a large blunt wooden needle and a small dish of colored beads.

"You can do it," Mrs Brice said. "Once you're started you'll see how easily it goes." Mrs Brice was well into her third, or possibly fourth, pair, and was thinking of switching to knotted belts.

Lottie did a little technical explaining, and soon had Mrs Judson hesitantly threading a thong through a hole.

"I love your painting," Mrs Brice said. "That's what I wish I could do. I can't even draw a straight line."

Lottie laughed. "If it depended on drawing straight lines I'd soon have to give up. They say the famous Italian painter Giotto proved his genius by picking up a brush and painting a *perfect* circle. Now that's something I could never do in a million years. It's more a matter of putting down the colors in different areas, so they approximate the mental picture you have in mind."

"What is the scene you're depicting?" Mrs Brice asked.

"It's a little place on Cape Cod where Norris and I sometimes go for his vacation. These are the dunes, and the sea of course, and the green bushes with pink flowers represent the wild rosa rugosas which flourish there. And this gray blob which is giving me such a hard time is the porch of the cottage where we stay. I'm sorely tempted to turn it into more dunes and roses."

"Oh don't," Mrs Brice said. "I can easily see it's a cottage—quite a cute one. It reminds me of our camp down at the lake. I wouldn't go there last summer—Thad had such fun, growing up on his vacations there. He had his own canoe. Now I may feel differently. The sunsets over the lake—our view is to the west—are lovely."

"I can imagine," Lottie said.

"Oh dear," Mrs Judson said, but this time Miss Pride beat Lottie to it.

"Here," she said. "You have the thong on that side, now you want to bring it back to this side. It's just like simple sewing."

"I never did learn to sew properly," Mrs Judson said. "The one task I dread is sewing the buttons back on Sam's shirts when they

(95)

come off in the laundry. I have a nice woman who does mending for me—like torn sheets, or the children's clothes when they were growing up. She's so fast, I marvel at it."

"Now that you've gotten it through there," Miss Pride said, "what are you going to do next?"

"Try and put it through that hole?" Mrs Judson asked.

"If you do that, won't you be skipping this hole?"

"I suppose so. Should I put it through there?"

"What do you think?"

"I honestly don't know, but I suppose I might as well try it. Yes, I can see how it looks like stitches. First one side, then the other."

Mr Mulwin appeared in the door. "Had to cut the swimming short. Fellow from another ward tried to drown himself. At any rate, he sank. Personally, I think he just wasn't much of a swimmer."

Lottie frowned unhearingly at her painting.

"Why Mr Mulwin," Miss Pride said, "can't we tempt you into joining us in one of our activities? How about a lovely knotted belt for Mrs Mulwin?"

"Who's this 'we'?" Mr Mulwin said.

"You're a tease," Miss Pride said. She was quite pretty with a nice smile. "Why don't you just let me show the simple principle of the thing. Here, you can pick out the colors."

Mr Mulwin shrugged. "Why not? It will sure stun Ethel if I make something in here. I've read all the magazines in the sun room. I don't like those colors. Haven't you got something less garish?"

"How about this dark red, with this brown? Just the two colors together would be very effective."

"OK. Now show me how it goes. I've tied trout flies, so this ought to be a snap."

"The important thing to remember is to keep the tension and make the knots really tight. Otherwise it doesn't come out looking so nice."

"I have strong hands," Mr Mulwin said, flexing them.

"What do you think of my painting, Mr Mulwin?" Lottie asked.

"Do you want my candid opinion?"

"Certainly."

"Not bad, for an amateur. But what's that gray blob on the left?"

"That," Lottie said, "is supposed to be a porch, and it's giving me a lot of trouble."

"Why don't you paint a white window frame on it? Then it would look more like a house."

"That's a thought. But the porch I have in mind has screens and no white window frames. Still, thanks for the suggestion."

"Think nothing of it." Miss Pride soon had Mr Mulwin seated at a frame, knotting away. He worked deftly and with speed.

"Now what do I do?" Mrs Judson asked.

Mrs Brice leaned over and considered her work. "You've done this side, now you want to do the other in the same way."

"Like this?"

"No. That will reverse the stitches. Put the thing—the thong—through from this side."

"I seem to be getting somewhere," Mrs Judson said, "but I haven't the least idea of what I'm doing. I don't suppose I'll ever finish them."

"You're going quite quickly," Mrs Brice said. "Just keep at it."

"Oh dear. Suppose I haven't finished these when my three months are up, do you think they wouldn't let me go home? I ache to give the downstairs a good turning out."

"Don't worry yourself needlessly," Lottie said. "You'll have those done in a few days. Anyway, we're not prisoners here. We're patients."

"Say, Mrs Taylor," Mr Mulwin said, "how about a martini, nice and dry and on the rocks? I could use one myself."

Lottie put down her brush. "Damn you," she said.

Mrs Brice bridled. "All I can say, Mr Mulwin," she said, "is that I pity your wife. From the bottom of my heart."

"Don't fret yourself about Ethel," Mr Mulwin said. "She can look out for herself. She can also take a little ribbing without going all to pieces."

Lottie left the room, but immediately returned, picked up her brush and went on painting. "They call it taking the rough with the smooth," she said.

Mrs Judson, who had been staring at Mr Mulwin's back in something between horror and terror, returned to her moccasin. Bertha

(97)

came in.

"Where's the modeling clay?" she said. "I want to mess around with it."

"It's there," Mis Pride said, "on the potter's wheel. Are you going to make a nice jug? Or perhaps a vase?"

"I'm not going to make anything. I'm just going to mess with it. It's healthy. It may come out an abstract, but I won't keep it. I don't believe in making things to keep, like moccasins. There are too many things in the world already."

"If it comes out an abstract," Miss Pride said, "you could glaze it and then I'd fire it in the kiln. It might be quite nice, a sculpture of your own making."

"No," Bertha said, "it's against my principles. Say, why can't we have a radio in here?"

"Good night shirt," Mr Mulwin said. "I came in here to get away from that phonograph. I'm going to ask them to make it a rule that it can only be played during certain specific hours. That's only fair to those who hate it."

"The great white hunter barks again," Bertha said. "I notice you don't mind sitting staring at those dumb TV shows all evening."

A creative silence invaded the room, and stayed for a while. Mrs Brice put down her handiwork and went to the table where Mr Mulwin was working. "Do you mind," she said, "if I watch for a minute? Maybe I could pick up the craft—I don't really need all these moccasins I'm making."

"I don't like anybody standing over me," Mr Mulwin said with his wonted grace.

"Perhaps if I just pulled up this chair? For a minute?" Mrs Brice said bravely. Lottie slipped her an encouraging smile.

"Suit yourself," he said.

"That's right," Bertha said. "This room is for everybody: he can't tell you where to sit, stand or lie down." Mrs Brice quietly seated herself and watched Mr Mulwin's flying fingers. "Say," Bertha continued to Mr Mulwin, "this is getting to look a lot like you." The lump of clay had acquired ears, nose and a chin. Mr Mulwin glanced up.

(98)

"No it doesn't," he said, "not in the least. If it's sculpture you're after, you've still got a long way to go, kid."

"I think I could learn to do it," Mrs Brice said, apropos the belt knotting, "but I wouldn't be nearly as good at it as you are."

"As I say," Mr Mulwin said, "I used to knot trout flies. That takes skill and patience, believe me."

"I thought," Lottie said, "that you never had time for recreation."

"Trout fly tying isn't recreation. It's craft—an art."

"When did you give up fly fishing?" Lottie asked.

"Would you mind not quizzing me? I'm trying to keep my mind on my work."

"I don't call what we do in here work," Lottie said. "I call it recreation. Though I may keep up my painting when I'm at home. I enjoy bringing an image out of nowhere, and the way the paints squoosh."

"You have a gift for it," Mrs Brice said. "You ought to keep it up: it would be a waste not to. I have a small confession. I've always known I wasn't a handy sort of person, and I didn't want to have anything to do with making things in craft therapy. But one day, after I'd been here a while, I came in to look around. There was a patient—she's left now—who had the most terrible shaky hands: palsy, I imagine. Anyway, she was sitting here, making a lovely pair of moccasins. I thought to myself, if that poor trembling creature can do it, well, then so can *I*. And I sat down and got right at it. You never know what's in you until you try."

Bertha laughed. "You're a heavy competitive type and you don't know it."

Mrs Brice thought before she spoke. "No, Bertha, I don't think it was competitiveness. I think that lady was more of an inspiration to me. Seeing her woke me up: I realized it was at least worth trying, even if I didn't have much faith in myself."

"There," Lottie said. The gray blob had become more porchlike, though it seemed somewhat to obtrude from the picture. "I can't honestly say I'm satisfied, but if I go on I'm afraid I'll only make it worse, not better."

"It's nice," Mrs Judson said. "I think I've gone wrong."

(99)

Miss Pride came over. "Yes, this is where you slipped up. You crossed over instead of going straight on to the next hole."

"Oh," Mrs Judson said.

"Let's see if you can't work it out," Miss Pride said. "Pull the thong out back to here."

"Do I have to undo all that work?" Mrs Judson asked.

"If you want to get it right: you do want to get it right, don't you?"

"I suppose so." Mrs Judson unlaced the thong to the place indicated and recommenced.

"Why Bertha," Miss Pride said, "that's most interesting." The clay head had taken on a slight resemblance to Mr Mulwin. At least, it had his bulbous nose and stick-out ears.

"No it isn't," Bertha said. "It's meant to be mean, but it's not meant to be interesting. When I'm through I'll mess it all up again."

"That," Mr Mulwin said, "does not bear the remotest resemblance to me, if that's your intention." He went on in a kindly voice, "You know, Bertha, you suffer from a peculiar psychological ailment, and it may well be incurable. You are a spoiled brat. That's it in a nutshell. What you need is a good hard job you have to go to every day. That would snap you out of it, if anything can."

"A good hard job? Is that what made you Mr Mental Health Week?"

"Would you mind letting me concentrate?" Mr Mulwin lamely replied.

"That's an interesting conception you've got there, Bertha," Lottie said, and giggled.

"I don't think we should descend to personalities," Mrs Brice said. "I can't tell you, Mr Mulwin, how I admire the way you go at that. Look how much you've already done."

"Thanks," Mr Mulwin said. "Glad to have at least one on my side."

"You must be very strong," Lottie said.

"You're darn tootin'. That's why that fresh la di da husband of yours had better watch his step. Or his language."

"Oh come now," Lottie said, "I thought we'd gotten beyond the threatened fisticuffs stage. Nobody likes to be threatened, including

Norris."

A nurse with a cart entered. "Medication," she said. "Mrs Taylor?" She extended a paper cup with two pills in it, and another of water.

Lottie sighed and tossed back the pills and took a swallow of water. "Thanks. My good old paraldehyde, how I miss it. I was high as a kite and I didn't even know it. Personally, I think these tranquilizers are just a lot of old aspirin, dressed up in pretty colors."

3

"I hate tapioca cream," Nick Tromper said.

"Then don't eat it," his mother said.

"Can Michael and I be excused?"

"Don't you want to let Michael finish his dessert? Down boy," she said to a dog of part Newfoundland descent. It had put its paws on the table and was investigating the possibilities of leftovers. The younger Tromper children were engaged in a game of 'I Spy With My Little Eye' in which Nick and Michael studiously refused to join.

"Hurry up," Nick said. Michael continued to eat at the rate enjoined at home.

"How's your father?" Mr Tromper asked. "I didn't see him at the V.F.W. the other evening."

"He's fine. I think he had to go out and play bridge. It made him kind of sore. Missing the V.F.W., I mean."

"And the others? Your grandmother?"

"They're all fine, too, thank you. Only Twing, our cat, got out and got into a fight and had to go to the vet. But she's back home now. She loves to fight."

"As I recall," Mr Tromper said, "Twing is a Siamese?"

"That's right."

"A pugnacious crew. Our animals are all highly hybrid, to say the least. Our house is a kind of animal orphanage—waifs and strays. But since Boxer is really Nick's dog, it only seemed fair for the rest of the troop to each have its own pet."

"Aren't you through yet?" Nick said to Michael.

"Almost."

"Perhaps Michael would like another helping. There's plenty."

"Well, all right, thank you." Michael passed his dish.

"Good grief," Nick said, "We'll be here all night."

"What are you planning that's so important," Mrs Tromper said, "if you don't mind my asking."

"We've got to study. Then maybe we'll fool around with the basketball. Or go uptown."

"If you go uptown, don't stay late. Remember."

"I never do. Well hardly ever. Just that once when I lost track of the time."

"You certainly did. I was worried sick."

The doorbell sounded and one of the younger children went and admitted Norris Taylor.

"I'm early," Norris said when he had divested himself of his topcoat. "You're still eating."

"Pull up a chair," Mr Tromper said. "We're just finishing up. Would you like a dish of dessert?"

"No thanks. Mrs Gompers leaves me such hearty meals I can hardly get through them. But I don't like to offend her by throwing out too much. She's been a rock of Gibraltar to me while Lottie's away."

"Mag should be along soon," Mrs Tromper said, "and we can get to the cards."

"I'm finished," Michael said.

"OK boys, scoot," Mrs Tromper said. Michael and Nick went up to Nick's room, which was decorated with posters and photographs of sports and rock stars.

"You sure do eat a lot," Nick said.

"I'm not a beanpole like you," Michael said. Nick was tall and thin and went out for basketball. The next hour and a half was spent in study, climaxed by wrestling match which Michael won, despite Nick's eel-like slitheriness.

"Why don't you sleep over here tonight?" Nick said.

"I'd have to call up and ask, and walk over and get my toothbrush and stuff. I don't know. Don't you have to ask your parents first?"

"No, not really. But I'll tell my mother. Say, I'll ask her to call up—that way your family's more likely to say yes. I've noticed your father's stricter than mine."

"My Dad's OK."

"Didn't say he wasn't. Come on."

At the bridge table Mrs Tromper was, by good fortune, dummy. "Why yes," she said, "that's a nice idea. I'll call Maureen right now."

She went into the hall and dialed the Delahantey residence. "Biddy? It's Gladys Tromper. How are you? Not that I need ask: you're always in wonderful health and spirits. Is Maureen there? Could I speak to her for a moment? Maureen? Gladys. The boys seem to think it would be a good idea if Michael slept over tonight, and it's fine with us. Heavens no. A boy more or less goes completely unnoticed around this house. I keep some spare tooth brushes—you know, the disposable kind they have in motels—just for occasions like this. And Michael can wear a pair of Nick's pajamas, if he doesn't try to button the jacket. You certainly have a stalwart pair. What. Oh. All right." She put her hand over the mouthpiece of the phone and said, "Your mother wants to speak to your father first. What's that, Maureen? Just a minute. Your father wants to know what about your music practice."

"I practiced this afternoon."

"He says he practiced this afternoon. It's all right then? Good. I'll see that they get to bed in decent time. I'm afraid we Trompers have a reputation for rather free and easy ways but I see to it that Nick gets his sleep. In fact, I couldn't keep him from it if I tried. He asked for special permission the other night to stay up and watch something on TV and in fifteen minutes he was out like a light in front of the set. It was too funny. How's Bryan? That's good. We must get together— now I have to get back to a bridge table and see how badly we went down. Let's see each other. Yes, soon. Goodnight." She hung up the phone and said, "That's all arranged. If you're going uptown, Nick knows what time to be back. Have you got your watch?"

"I have mine," Michael said.

"Well, have fun. Did we make it or were we set?" Gladys called as she returned to the living room. The chairs not occupied by the players were taken by animals, whose number seemed much greater than five.

Nick and Michael walked uptown to the Main Street, where they joined some other boys standing under a street lamp. Here they stayed for half an hour or more, exchanging views and ribaldries, (someone called Michael, "The Crisco Kid, fat in the can," for which Michael gave him a good clout), then strolled back to the Tromper home.

They were discussing ambitions. "My Dad would like it," Nick said, "if one of us became a C.P.A. like him."

"What's that?"

"Certified Public Accountant. You can make a good living at it, but I don't know. A desk job. I might like to be something more outdoors, like a firewarden in a forest somewhere. Only you're alone an awful lot. I'm not used to that."

"At least you have a room of your own. I've always had to share one with Patrick. I'm *never* alone. I wouldn't know what it was like."

"Yeah, I'm lucky," Nick said, "that we live in this big old house. I guess it's kind of a mess, but at least I don't have to bunk in with one of the brats. My mother isn't like yours, mine hates housework. But she does pretty good considering. Your house is like a museum, it's so perfect."

"My mother likes things just so, I guess is the reason. She and my father always get together and pick out exactly the thing they want, then they won't accept any substitutes."

"Your family is strict. You and Patrick never come uptown in the evening, like the other guys."

"It's the way my father was brought up. My mother's more liberal—if it was just left up to her we could run around more. But my Dad—boy. He gave Patrick an awful crack the other evening because he sassed him. For a minute I thought Patrick was going to take him—he could, too. Patrick's even stronger than I am. Can you keep a secret?"

"Sure."

"Patrick says if he ever hits him again, he's going to run away.

(104)

Actually, he said he's going to *move* away. He can pass for a lot older than his age. I bet what he'd do is lie about his age and enlist in the Marines. He's always been hipped on the Marines."

"Oh wow. Nobody in my family ever hit me. Except once when I was a little kid I got my hand slapped for fooling with the gas range. But that was for my own protection. I turned on all the burners and nearly blew the house up. Or asphyxiated everybody. I don't think Patrick would really do that, do you?"

"Yes, I do. I have a feeling though that afterwards Mom talked to Dad hard about how we're too big to slap around. He has a bad temper, but he listens to her. She doesn't lay down the law so much, but when she does, she means it."

When the boys got back to the house the bridge game was just breaking up, but they managed to slip upstairs without having to mix it up with their elders. After washing, brushing their teeth and a lot of joking about the way Nick's pajamas fitted Michael, they got into bed.

"Oh man, I could sleep for a month," Nick said. He was soon dead asleep. The libidinous Michael pretended to fall asleep too, then tried a little gentle pressure with his knee, as though shifting. Nick pulled his legs up sharply. After a while Michael rolled over and, eventually, fell into a deep sleep himself.

Somewhat later, Norris opened Mag Carpenter's front door, locked it behind him and stole upstairs. Mag was in bed.

"Help," she said, "it's an intruder."

"Precisely what I plan to do to you," Norris said. "Intrude."

"Coarse. There's your coat hanger and here's your drink. Or would you prefer to sit over there and we can review the bridge game?"

"Just let me get out of these tight shoes," Norris said, "and we'll see how you are at gin rummy."

"Sweetheart. And don't turn your back when you take your pants off."

"Don't worry. I'll be turning around any year now."

Chapter VII

1

"Do you have a piece of paper, an envelope and a stamp I could borrow?" Bertha asked of Lottie. "And a pen."

"Certainly. Only you needn't borrow them. Take them as a little gift."

"No. I'll pay you back. Sometime. It's a matter of principle. When I get outdoor privileges I'll go to the gift shop and get some supplies. Note paper and stuff. Then I'll write to my so-called friends at the college and see if they're too chicken to write back. It will be an experiment."

"I see," Lottie said, and went and fetched the needed articles from her room. Bertha put on the phonograph (although elsewhere in the sun room, a small group was watching TV), sat down at a card table and stared at the sheet of paper some time. Then she went over to Lottie and asked her the date. When she learned it, she returned to her table and wrote it down. Then she wrote, "Dear", and paused again. After rejecting different terms, she made this into "Dear

Family." It took a long time, though the letter was short. When she finished she took it to Lottie.

"Like to read what I wrote?"

"If it's nothing too personal," Lottie said. She was crocheting afghan squares.

"Not personal at all." Lottie took the note and read,

Dear Family,

After thinking it over a lot I decided it is alright for you to come to my evening group. Get in touch with the doctor for further details. He will tell you when.
           Sincerely yours
           Your Daughter Bertha

"I think," Lottie said, "this is a wise decision. And that it shows what progress you have made."

Bertha, who was doing her shuffling dance, said, "Dr Kearney made it pretty plain I'd better shape up and ask them. They're holding a long term hospital over my head as a threat. The Hartford Retreat, or some place like that. No, thank you."

"I'm sure they wouldn't do a thing like that unless they were certain it was for your ultimate good."

"Oh, if they dish it out, I can take it. Probably there'd at least be some kids my age. Here, everybody's practically a grandparent. No offense."

"I suppose I could be a grandparent," Lottie said, "but only just. And Mr Mulwin must be in his thirties—though I suppose to you that seems quite old enough."

"Did you hear Meanie Mulwin is going to get electric shock? They can't get through his depression pattern with the medication. He must have a will of iron, the way he absolutely won't change at all."

"Lately," Lottie said, "while I wouldn't call him Sweetness and Light, I've had the feeling he was silently reaching out for some kind of companionship, or sympathy. Of course if anyone responds, he tends to react in his customary way. The idea of shock frightens me.

(108)

I'm glad I didn't have it."

"I had it in the first hospital I was in," Bertha said. "It didn't do any good. Not long anyhow."

Mrs Brice, looking trim in green, got up from her chair and joined them. "I never thought," she said, "I'd end my days watching daytime movies on TV in a psychiatric institute. Tarzan. Imagine. Lottie, do you feel up to a stroll about the grounds?"

"Why, yes, I believe I do. Just let me put away my busy work and get a jacket. I think it's cooler out than it looks."

"Wish I could come," Bertha said.

"I'm sure they'll soon give you outdoor privileges," Mrs Brice said, as she waited for Lottie.

"Not yet awhile they won't. They know I'd run away. Which would be dumb, because I haven't got any place to run away to. Still, I'd do it. When I feel an impulse, I go right ahead and do it. Guess that's why I'm here. But I'd rather be a creature of impulse than a human vegetable." Bertha regarded Mrs Judson, who was now sitting alone, staring at the TV, which exhibited a string of familiar commercials.

"Mrs Judson," Mrs Brice said, "is not a vegetable. She's every bit as much a person as you or I. I'm surprised to hear you talk that way about someone so kind."

"I'm like old Mulwin," Bertha said. "I have a mean streak. I don't like to bottle it up or it will eat my vitals away. And where would I be without my vitals?"

"I think you're more of a tease than you are mean," Mrs Brice said.

Lottie approached, having put on a light knitted jacket. "Ready?" she said.

"All set," Mrs Brice said. They signed out at the desk, and passing through several tiled corridors, reached the doors. The sun was out, the grounds immaculately kept.

"This is lovely," Lottie said. "We should take more advantage of these balmy days. Shall we stroll, or shall we have a goal?"

"Why don't we go to the gift shop? I don't think I want to buy anything, but it gives me the feeling I'm going shopping."

"Yes, I like that too. I can hardly wait to get back to my dear old

(109)

supermarket and a shopping cart. I like to keep a full larder. Norris sometimes has some quite odd requests at bedtime, in the way of a sandwich or bowl of soup."

"I like a full larder too," Mrs Brice said. "I like to open the door and see it all there, in rows. In the cellar we have a special cupboard for the home canning. At the end of the season, it used to be my pride and joy, the jams, the jellies, tomato conserve—I even had my own secret recipe for piccalilli, a favorite of Mr Brice's. Of course after Thad grew up, there wasn't the need—how that boy loved jelly on his sandwiches, with peanut butter—and I tapered off. This year I didn't do any conserving at all. Mr Brice asked if I wouldn't just do a little strawberry jam, and maybe some rhubarb for pies, but at the time I couldn't bring myself to take the interest. This year I'll do a little, the two of us don't need much."

"I've never been a heavy canner," Lottie said, "there's always been just Norris and myself. But I do like to do a few special jams and jellies. Like apple mint, to go with the ham. One year in a fit of ambition, I made my own mince meat. It was a tremendous amount, I thought we'd never see the end of it. Whisky. There was whisky in it. Well, I won't be making that again. Though I suppose I could eat a wedge of mince pie without running amok. Maybe."

The breeze moved the trees and the leaf shadows trembled on the walks and lawns. It was a dream-like afternoon as they strolled on. At the gift shop they inspected the familiar wares. Many, like the giant stuffed pandas, were intended as gifts for children in other parts of the giant complex of the hospital. Lottie frowned at the skimpy selection of cosmetics, and finally picked out a lipstick and bought it. "Shall we go?" she said, then realized that Mrs Brice was on the verge of tears. When they were outside again in the sun the tears flowed. Mrs Brice dabbed at them with a Kleenex and Lottie took her arm and remained silent.

After awhile, Mrs Brice said, "It was a teddy bear. I once bought one just like it."

"I thought it was something like that," Lottie said. "I spend so much time feeling sorry for myself, then I realize what's happened to someone like you, and I feel ashamed of myself. Why don't we sit on this bench and just enjoy the sun?"

They did so, and Mrs Brice became calm again. "What did you buy" she asked.

Lottie showed her the lipstick, a rather girlish pink, and said, "I don't need it, dear knows, but I thought a slight change of decor might perk me up."

When they returned to the ward, they passed Mr Mulwin in the corridor. He was being wheeled to his room on a cot, and seemed unconscious, although his eyes were partly open. Mrs Judson passed too at that moment, averted her eyes, and said, "Oh dear."

Lottie went to her room, sat down in front of the mirror and combed and smoothed her hair. She wiped off the lipstick she was wearning and started to apply the new shade. Bertha came to the door. Lottie frowned at the interruption.

"You know that letter?"

"Yes."

"The one I showed you?"

"What about the letter, Bertha?"

"I didn't send it."

"Was that wise? I think you should have." Lottie continued to study her lips.

"You never know when the nurses will get around to mailing the letters you give them," Bertha said. "They take all day about it. The letter might even get lost. I wouldn't put it past them."

"My mail comes and goes quite promptly," Lottie said. "I don't think you need be so distrustful."

"Well, I am. So I called them up instead. I got my dopey brother first, but then he put my mother on. She sounded happy to hear my voice, just like those telephone company ads—'call up a loved one tonight.' This way, they'll be able to come to a session sooner and I'll get out of here quicker. I'm not so dumb as I look. Do you think I look dumb?"

"No, not at all. Just a shade too self-absorbed at times."

"When you're not sweet, I know what you're thinking about."

"Well, don't say it and we'll continue to be friends. What do you think of this shade of lipstick. Do you think it's too young for me?"

"It looks OK. I don't believe in make-up myself. It's false and anti-nature."

"The natural look is all very well at your age, Bertha. But at mine, a little help is more than welcome."

"A lot of women your age don't wear make-up."

"I've noticed. It's simply not my style. If I were more of an outdoor person I might pull my hair back in a bun and have that tanned leathery look. But I'm not. The telephone. Do you know, that gives me an idea. Excuse me." Lottie left her room and went to the pay phone in the corridor and called Norris at his office, a thing she rarely did.

"This is a pleasant surprise," Norris said, when she was put through. He was going over Mag Carpenter's will with her. The will was composed of a myriad little bequests to charities and distant cousins, and Norris had been reasoning with her about dropping some of the charities, and leaving larger sums to a few.

"Norris," Lottie said, "I have a favor to ask."

"Ask away, I am yours to command."

"Would you have the florist send a plant to Mr Mulwin for me?"

"Am I dreaming?"

"No, you're not. Have the card say, 'With best wishes, from a friend.' To Mr Gregory Mulwin. You know the address. All too well."

"I also know him. I should think he might throw it out. Or suspect a plot."

"You don't understand. He's just had electric shock treatment, and they say when he comes out of the after effects, he'll be quite a different person. He'll probably think it's from someone where he works, or a neighbor, but that's all right. I sense that he'll be in a receptive mood, and enjoy receiving it. Somehow today I'm very aware of how important it is that we help each other when we can, in these little ways."

"My dear, you're very kind. Of course I'll do it."

"Everything all right there at the office?"

"Everything is much as usual, which passes for all right."

"Then I'll see you this evening—no, it's tomorrow evening. I won't keep you any longer. Remember, his first name is Gregory."

"Will do. In fact, I've already made a note of it." They bade their goodbyes.

"Was that Lottie?" Mag asked.

"Yes, it was. Now before we get back to this codicil about the Community Chest, I have a call to make. I must call a florist."

"You've never sent me flowers."

"Nor, my dear, am I going to start."

2

"Well, Nick," Bryan Delehantey said, "you've certainly become a long drink of water."

"It's funny," Nick said. "Nobody else in my family is extra tall. My Dad's not short, but he's not tall either. I don't mind it: I like basketball."

"Hi Nick," Patrick said, coming into the living room.

"And where were you?" Bryan said.

"He's been being a good lad," Biddy said, "and running an errand for your old mother. Did they match the wool?"

"I think so," Patrick said. "Here it is." He handed her a bag.

"Yes," Biddy said. "That's right. I do love a nice rich dark red. It goes with everything." She regarded the maroon hanks Patrick had gotten for her. "Who would like to volunteer his hands while I wind this yarn?"

Neither twin spoke and Nick said, "I'll do it."

"No, Nick," Bryan said, "you're a guest. Let Patrick do it."

"But I just went all the way uptown to get the stuff," Patrick protested.

"It wouldn't seem so far uptown," Bryan said, "if it was a matter of hanging around the Candy Kitchen. However, in simple justice, Michael can do it." Bryan was in a mellow mood, having had an extra highball before dinner, which had been late.

Maureen looked in the room. "Whose turn is it to load the dishwasher? They're all cleared and rinsed and waiting."

"Michael's," Patrick said.

"Like heck it is. I did it last night. Anyway, I'm helping Gran."

"Come along Patrick, and stop fibbing." Maureen left the room followed by her lumbering son.

"Mr Delehantey," Nick asked, "would it be OK if the boys went uptown with me for a little while? We want to talk to some of the guys."

"'Fraid not, Nick. Homework and practicing. There's no point in their being in the school orchestra if they don't practice. Not that it doesn't make this house a merry hell."

"But it's Friday night," Michael protested. "And we practiced this afternoon like you asked us to, so it wouldn't get on your nerves."

Bryan expanded, "I'll admit I did forget there for a moment that it's Friday. It's my day off tomorrow, too, don't forget, and I'm not making any special event out of it."

"All we'd do," Michael said, "is walk uptown, have a coke and talk to the guys a little. The senior track meet is tomorrow afternoon— we're not in it but we'd like to go. Maybe you'd like to come too?"

"Maybe. Doubt if I'll have the time. Now if I let you go uptown, and say I expect you back at a reasonable hour, do I have to say precisely what time I mean?"

"No, sir," Michael said.

"And what hour do you have in mind?" Bryan asked.

"Ten o'clock?"

"Nine thirty. At the latest."

"But it's already eight o'clock."

"Do you want me to change my mind?" Bryan asked rhetorically.

"No, sir."

Eventually the wool was wound, the dishwasher loaded and the three boys set out. They had barely hit the sidewalk when Nick said, "Pete Petrosian has some great grass. His brother gave it to him when he was home from college last weekend. His brother is a great guy. Pete promised to bring a couple of joints."

"You can't stand around in front of the Candy Kitchen smoking grass," Patrick said.

"Don't be a jerk. We'll stroll over to the athletic field. That way, you can see if anybody's coming and the smell clears off in the air."

"I don't know," Patrick said.

"You've never smoked any," Michael said. "You're scared."

"Neither have you."

"Yes I have. Well, I didn't smoke it—Nick and I ate some and listened to records at his house. It was great. It really changes the music, so you can make out all the notes and hear the words. I wish we could smoke it where there's a record player. Guess I'll have to groove on the stars instead."

"I don't know," Patrick said, "if I want to get into dope."

"It's not dope—it's not addicting, I mean," Nick said. "It's a nice kick. The important thing is not to be scared of it, then you'll get relaxed and enjoy it."

"Somebody at school was smoking it in the can the other day," Michael said. "You could even smell it in the hall."

"How do you know how it smells?" Patrick said.

"I could guess. It's a special smell. You'll see."

"It must have been that lunkhead Luke," Nick said. "He's bad news. He'll take any crazy chances—and I've heard about the way he drives when he's drunk or stoned. He's going to wind up in the morgue or jail or out on his butt. I'm glad I'm not old enough to be in his crowd. And does he ever play dirty basketball!"

"Yeah," Patrick said. "I've noticed."

In front of the Candy Kitchen they joined Pete Petrosian and a couple of other youths.

"Got it?" Nick asked.

Pete touched the breast pocket of his shirt.

"Well?" Nick said. "Why don't we amble over to the athletic field and set the world on fire?"

"What's the rush?" Pete said. "I kind of like it here."

"The twins have to go home real soon. You know how strict their Dad is," Nick said.

"Yeah," Patrick said, "he is pretty strict."

"He wasn't so bad tonight," Michael said. "At any rate, we're here."

After some more palaver, the group set off for the athletic field, an

(115)

open space between the park and the highschool, with bleachers and a track.

"I better explain to you guys how to smoke this," Pete said. "Take a drag, pull some air in with it and suck it down into your lungs. Hold it there, then let it out slow through your head and nose. This is good stuff my brother gave me, so it won't take much to turn you on."

"I don't know," Patrick muttered. Pete took a joint out of his pocket, lit it and passed it around. When it came to Patrick, he took it and inhaled deeply, then had a coughing fit. Michael was more expert. On the second joint, Patrick did better, inhaling deeply and keeping the oddly scented smoke in his lungs a long time. He exhaled, feeling slightly lightheaded. After what seemed a very long or else a very short time, he looked up and saw the stars stagger in their courses.

"Jesus," he said and sat down hard. Nick went off into spasms of silent laughter.

"You all right, brother buddy?" Michael asked. He extended his arms and said, "I'm a kite and I'm flying."

"That's the idea," Pete said. "Groove with it. Look: it's like you can see right around the high school, all four sides at once."

"I'm going to lie here," Patrick said. The stars slowed down and seemed individually to glitter and smile down on his young face. "I don't know if I like it or not. I'm not sure. I just can't tell. You ought to lie down and dig the stars. Did you know that infinity has no end? It just goes on and on and on and on."

"He's starting to rap," Pete said.

"I'm on top of the world," Michael said. "The whole world comes to a point in this athletic field, and I'm the one who's on top of it."

"I wish we had a transistor with us," Nick said. "I'd like to hear some music." He began to sing a pop song, off-key.

"Holy shit," Patrick said. "It must be midnight. Dad will skin us alive,."

"We haven't been here fifteen minutes," Pete said. "Look." He held out his wristwatch which had a luminous dial. It was indeed still early.

"I don't know," Patrick said. "I think we better get home."

"First you better see if you can get off your back and walk."

"A shooting star!" Patrick said. "I saw a shooting star."

"Where?" Nick said.

"There," Patrick said. "In the sky."

"When you think about it," Michael said, "it's great, being a part of the universe."

3

"Do you know what I miss?" Lottie asked. She and Norris were strolling down the corridor to the room where family group was held.

"I never was any good at mind reading," Norris said, "and it gets worse as I get older."

Lottie lifted her head to his ear and whispered, "B-e-d, bed." Norris gave her arm a hard affectionate squeeze. "It won't be so long now," he said.

The others were already assembled around the table when the Taylors came in, closely followed by Dr Kearney. Mr Mulwin looked pale. Good-evenings were exchanged between the patients and the visitors. Behind Bertha sat a pleasant-looking couple, who were introduced as Mr and Mrs Hartz, her parents.

"I see, Bertha," Dr Kearney said, "you finally took the giant step."

"Sure," Bertha said. "Why not?"

"No reason that I ever knew of," Dr Kearney said.

"I was mad at them for putting me in here, among other things," Bertha said. "I think that was it."

"We're glad to see you looking so well, dear," Mrs Hartz said. "Your brother sent his love."

"I'll bet he did."

"Perhaps what he actually said was, 'Say hello to Bertha,' but I knew what he meant. A boy his age isn't apt to be demonstrative."

"How are you feeling, Mr Mulwin?" Lottie asked.

"Sapped. Or maybe I mean zapped. It's like I don't know what hit me, although of course I do know. How do you feel?"

"Better," Lottie said. "Not so shaky and driven. But I still get the craving. Not so often as before."

"Did you send me a plant?" Mr Mulwin asked her.

"As a matter of fact, I did." Mrs Mulwin frowned slightly.

"I figured as much. Nobody else would I could think of. Thanks."

"You're very welcome. The men's bedrooms look so cheerless from the hall, while all the women's have flowers in them."

"What kind of a plant is it?" Mr Mulwin asked.

"An azalea," Norris said.

"Oh, were you in on this too?"

"Just as an agent for my wife. She isn't allowed off the grounds to go to a florist's. You'd think they'd have a flower shop in the hospital: it would certainly show a profit."

"That's right," Mr Mulwin said. "It would make somebody a nice little business."

"Business, business," Mrs Judson said. "I'm getting fed up, hearing about business. It's all you men seem to think about."

"Why Ethel," Sam Judson said, "at home you always took a real interest in my work and how it was going."

"That was different," Mrs Judson said. "That was at home. Now I'm stuck here, making moccasins nobody needs."

"You might make me a pair," Sam said. "I could wear them around the house. Like slippers."

"And when I've made those, then what? I want to go home."

"And I want you at home. You're beginning to open up," Sam said. "Although I've never heard you talk in this cross way before."

"Somebody went through my dresser drawers. I suspect *you*," Ethel Judson said to Bertha.

"You're full of baked beans," Bertha said. "What could possibly be in your dresser that would faintly intrigue me? An elastic stocking?"

"Now you're making fun of my varicose veins. You're awful. None of my children were brats like you, heavens be thanked."

"I've never met you before," Mrs Hartz said, "but I'll thank you not to call my daughter a brat. She's had problems, as you yourself apparently have."

"That's right," Mr Hartz backed up his wife, "Bertha isn't a brat."

"Oh blah," Mrs Judson said, and fell silent.

"Go ahead," Bertha said. "Let it out. I can take it. All you sweet old ladies, full of venom and bile."

"Sincerely," Mrs Brice said, "I don't think I'm full of venom and vile. I mean, bile. I don't think Mrs Judson is either: the hospital and not being in your own home and all can get on anybody's nerves. It does mine sometimes. I look forward to going home."

"And I look forward to having you home again, mother. It's a lonely place without you."

"I'm sorry you don't want to hear about business, Mrs Judson," Mr Mulwin said, "because that's what I'm in here about: too much business, too many business worries, wondering if I could trust my managers all the way. Of course you can't, it's putting temptation in a man's path."

"Say," Bertha said, "just what is your line of business."

"I have a chain of drugstores."

"How big a chain?" Bertha demanded.

"We have three branches, plus the main outlet down on State Street."

"What's it called? I never heard of any drugstore around here called Mulwin's."

"The Thrifty Drug Company."

"Oh that," Bertha said. "I've been in one of those. The doctor gave me a prescription for some kind of uppers when I had the downs. I got it filled in one of your stores. They weren't any good. Too mild. No kick, no boost, no up."

"We just fill the prescriptions as the doctors write them. He probably didn't believe in anything too stimulating. Lots of doctors don't. It depends on the patient. I used to help myself to a little benzedrine when I didn't feel up to snuff."

"Benzedrine," Dr Kearney said, "can make a person touchy—in fact more than touchy, downright paranoid. That may have been a precipitant of the condition that brought you here."

"I wasn't hooked on the stuff," Mr Mulwin said. "Just now and then. Mostly I've got more energy than I need. Nervous energy."

(119)

"Do you need a prescription to get amyl nitrite?" Bertha asked.

"You do indeed," Mr Mulwin said. "Nor have you any need for it unless you have a heart condition."

"Poppers," Bertha said. "They have their uses—at the right time."

"I'm afraid," Mrs Hartz said, "that at college Bertha was led to experiment with drugs."

"Nobody had to lead me," Bertha said. "Don't blame me on others. Besides, I never got into the hard stuff. I'm too smart to wind up a junkie."

"Of course you are, dear," her mother said. "I didn't mean to make any serious implications."

"I thought you said you'd tried LSD," Lottie asked. "Doesn't that count as hard stuff?"

"Not like heroin or coke or morphine or like that," Bertha said. "LSD and peyote are just mind extenders. Sunshine pills."

"I beg to differ," Dr Kearney said. "There are clinics chock-a-block with experiments with these so-called perception extenders. Some of them are sent so far out they never come back. They've been warned, but they won't believe it."

"I'm as much of a drug addict as Bertha ever was—not that she was really an *addict*. I suppose," Lottie said to Mr Mulwin, "I'll be going to one of your stores for my Antabuse tablets when I leave here. I couldn't bear having the prescription filled at our local pharmacy. Not that everyone doesn't know all about me already."

"You exaggerate," Norris said. "And those that do know only feel sympathy. You have had visitors, and flowers and letters. It will all soon be forgotten."

"Antabuse?" Mrs Brice said. "What's that?"

"It's a pill," Lottie said. "And after you take one, if you have a drink it makes you violently ill. Attractive thought. It will be my little invisible crutch."

Mrs Brice now turned to Dr Kearney. "When I leave here and stop my medication, mayn't I relapse. Sink back into my old depression."

"First of all, we'll hope you've become insightful enough that that won't happen. Secondly, your medication will continue for a time after you leave. Thirdly, you'll be coming in for consultations on a

(120)

diminishing schedule. Does that reassure you?"

"It will be funny," Mrs Brice said, "coming back as a visitor. Almost as funny as going home. I've gotten used to it here. To the routine, anyway."

"I agree," Lottie said. "I've kind of subsided into the routine here—no lists to make, no vacuum cleaner, no dishwasher to unload in the morning. I'm a scrupulous housekeeper—too scrupulous for some, I can't bear to see a thing out of place—but I wonder how I'll feel about it when I get home. It may merely seem a burden."

"You'll probably plunge into it like a seal into a pool," Mr Mulwin said, with sudden poetry.

"That's one thing my wife and I have always had in common," Norris said. "We're both fanatically tidy."

"Nothing wrong with that," Mr Mulwin said. "I had to let one man go: his store just wasn't orderly enough to meet my standards, which are high. A drugstore has to be kept scrupulously clean, or who would ever want to go into it?"

"I wouldn't," Mrs Brice said. "I like a nice clean shiny store. I stopped going to one shop because I could smell that they'd been using roach spray. 'No thank you,' I thought, and quietly went elsewhere. It was a handy delicatessen for little last minute purchases, but I'd rather walk a few more blocks and shop someplace you could see was kept clean."

"You see?" Mr Mulwin said, as though someone had challenged Mrs Brice. "Christ, I'm sleepy. Pardon the language."

"That will wear off," Dr Kearney said. "Only yesterday you were out like a light."

"I don't want that again if I can help it," Mr Mulwin said. "At the last minute I thought I was being murdered, or at least that I'd die and suffer terrible pain. It was a minute of pure terror. I never want to feel that again."

"It seems to have helped, though," Mrs Mulwin said.

"Oh, I'm no different than I ever was. Only I'm overcome with sleepiness. Could I be excused from this and go to bed?"

"Why don't you stick it out?" Dr Kearney said. "It won't be much longer, and you'll have a feeling of accomplishment."

(121)

"I've already got that. I built my business up from scratch with my own two hands. That's accomplishment."

"Yes," Lottie said. "That's real accomplishment. I've come to admire you."

"Business, business," Mrs Judson said. "There's got to be more to life than dishes and business."

"Hear, hear," Bertha said.

"There, there," Lottie said. "Different people have different objectives in life. What's yours, Bertha?"

"To get out of here."

"You can be more serious than that. I mean in a larger, life-scale sense."

"Your own objectives don't sound so hot to me," Bertha said. "Get off the sauce and keep dusting. That's not for me: I like dust. I might go to one of those free form colleges up in Vermont or New Hampshire, if my folks will give me an allowance. I can't make life plans in a nut house: I'm disconnected from my peer group."

"Of course," Mr Hartz said, "we'd like you to continue your education. I, personally, would like to feel a little more secure about your attitude towards drugs, even the so-called mild ones. It seems plain they don't agree with you."

"I'm not hooked on anything. I told you that. I told everybody that, and it's true."

"I think what your father means," Lottie said, "is more that you have experimented, and he'd like to feel that that period is behind you."

"Not even a joint now and then, to relax and groove on the music?"

"Marijuana," Dr Kearney said, "definitely does not agree with everyone, no matter how the popular legend goes."

Lottie giggled. "I wonder how it would affect me? It might be a good substitute for alcohol."

"Where are you planning to buy it?" Norris said. "I decline to meet some contact downtown and travel around with my briefcase full of contraband."

"You needn't worry, dear," Lottie said. "I'm not planning to spend my time sitting around the house—stoned, do they call it?"

(122)

"That's the word," Bertha said.

"You're an entire youthquake unto yourself, aren't you Bertha," Norris said.

"You wouldn't expect me to have the problems of middle aged and elderly depressives, would you? Where would be the sense in that?"

"Obviously," Norris said, "you're much better than you were, yet your dominant attitude still seems one of defiance. You keep stepping on your own shoe laces, so to speak. Like your experiments with drugs: surely you see how much harm they did you?"

"Smoking grass isn't an experiment, it's a trip. It's an experience. I don't intend to drop any more acid—take LSD to you, that is—I've had that. Besides, I don't believe in synthetics. Grass is organic."

"So is opium," Dr Kearney said, "from which the lethal heroin is derived."

"I've never fooled with that, and I'm not going to. You sound like I can't trust myself: I told you, I'm no junkie."

"When it isn't business, it's drugs," Mrs Judson said. "I never heard anything like it in my life. I'm that disgusted."

"I'm not disgusted," Lottie said. "I find this variety of human experience fascinating. And I've learned a lot of little things here that may add up to one big thing. I found out I could go without paraldehyde when I thought I couldn't. And I may make painting a serious hobby. I'll always be an amateur, but that's all right. The time flies by when I'm at my easel."

"I think your pictures are lovely," Mrs Brice said.

"Would you like to have one? Pick out the one you like best, and I'll make you a present of it."

"How sweet! And I know just the one I'll pick: that floral study you finished yesterday."

"That one? All right. It's yours."

"So you think my sitting up and listening to this is doing me some kind of good, hunh?" Mr Mulwin said with a touch of his old ardor to Dr Kearney. "OK. I'll go through with it."

"Your willingness to stay," Lottie said, "means you're playing a part in our little community, even if you don't feel up to participating this evening."

(123)

"I'm inclined to say, 'Oh balls,' " Mr Mulwin said. "I'll admit that right now I don't give a damn if my business goes to hell in a bobsled."

"You'll change your mind about that," Mrs Mulwin said. "You're tired, and that's not your basic character speaking."

"Then I'll shut up, like Mrs Judson."

"Don't tell me to shut up, you rude thing," Mrs Judson said.

"That's not what he meant," Sam Judson said.

"I guess I can hear as good as the next one," Mrs Judson said. "And I certainly won't shut up if I don't feel like it. How come Mrs Brice and Mrs Taylor can go trotting all over the grounds and I can't? I'm tired of being shut up in here. I need fresh air, too."

"All in good time," Dr Kearney said. "I understood you to say in our conference that if you went out you would take a bus straight back to your house."

"I wouldn't now. Sam would just bring me back to the hospital. I guess if these other grouches can stick it out, I can too."

"Would you like to have grounds privileges tomorrow?" Dr Kearney said.

"Nobody would go with me," Mrs Judson said, "and you're not allowed out alone." This was greeted by a massive protest of willingness to accompany Mrs Judson on her first stroll.

Even Mr Mulwin said, "I'd go with you, if I had grounds privileges and wasn't so damn sleepy. First they knock you out, then they tell you to stay awake when there's nothing to stay awake about."

"You may have privileges sooner than you think," Dr Kearney said.

"Probably it will rain," Mr Mulwin said.

"There's nothing wrong with that," Lottie said. "I quite enjoy a walk in the rain—not in a downpour, of course."

"I haven't got my rain hat here," Mr Mulwin said. "It's at home."

"I'll drop it off tomorrow, Greg," Mrs Mulwin said, "on my way to the store."

"Are you a partner in your husband's business?" Norris asked.

"No, but I'm keeping an eye on things for him while he's here. I'm a licensed pharmacist—that was how we met. Greg used to be my employer."

"Now she's the boss," Mr Mulwin said good-naturedly.

Chapter VIII

1

"Why look who's here," Biddy said to Maureen, who was wheeling a cart down an aisle of the supermarket.

"Hi, you two," Mag Carpenter said. "Now my secret is out," she said, regarding her own cart. "I like a glass of beer as a nightcap."

"I wouldn't mind that myself," Maureen said, "but with my girth, I don't dare to tackle beer."

"Maureen," Biddy said, "makes a delicious dish of shrimps cooked in beer. All the alcohol cooks out—otherwise I wouldn't set lip to it."

"Mercy," Mag said, "what a quantity of groceries you do have to buy. Those growing boys! So far, I've held off from the temptation of frozen dinners. Though cooking for one seems a little silly, it takes a bit more time, and I don't like the idea of slipping into sloppy habits. I make a point of keeping to the schedule Bartram and I evolved over the years."

"Yes," Biddy said, "that's the way. Keep going straight ahead. When I get up and put the kettle on every morning, it may seem I'm doing it for the family, but really I'm just following the habit I formed for my late lamented and my own family. Though if it gives Maureen and Bryan a couple of extra minutes in bed, I'm glad. My time is pretty much my own, and my days don't run me ragged the way they do them. Those two boys alone are a handful. I'm glad I don't have the bringing up of them; though at times I try to pour a little oil on troubled waters."

Maureen laughed heartily. "Biddy, I don't know where I'd be without you. You help out in hundreds of ways, always making a pie or a nice frosted cake. Our desserts are almost exclusively *her* province," she added to Mag.

"And you have the figure of a young woman!" Mag said, and blushed, as she inadvertently glanced at Maureen's ample form.

"Have you heard the news? About Lottie?" Maureen asked.

"Why no. I've been meaning to visit her again, but I get stuck in my own little rut. What's the news? Is she much better?"

"Better enough that she's to have a weekend pass, I think they call it, and come back to her own home for two days. Norris must be in seventh heaven—no bachelor, he."

"Now isn't that marvelous! Isn't that wonderful! I can't think of any news I'd rather hear."

"I should think," Maureen said, "that it must mean the end of her stay there is well in sight. She's a good neighbor—I've missed her."

"Oh, Mary Charlotte Taylor is one in a million," Mag said. "I don't know how the garden club could get along without her. I wonder if she'll go out to cocktail parties? I suppose so. It's probably one of the things they teach them in there: how to say, 'No, thank you' and ask for a ginger ale or something like that."

"Doubtless," Maureen said, "though I don't think I'll welcome her home with a cocktail party in her honor."

"Don't mind me," Mag said, "I'm such a rattle, I simply can't help looking on all sides of a question. Not that Lottie's a *question*. When I have them to dinner, I suppose I'll have to forego my little glass of sherry—or would that be rude to Norris? I guess I'll play it by ear and cross the bridge when I come to it."

"Bryan has a business acquaintance in A.A. and he urges other people to drink. I mean, if they normally drink, then go ahead and drink. He says it doesn't bother him at all. I suppose he feels a surge of confidence when he finds he can go without it."

"Giving things up is very good for building character," Biddy said.

"How true," Mag said. "And now I must be trundling on—fun running into you like this. We must see more of each other."

Purchases paid for, Mag went home and had hysterics, while the two Mrs Delahanteys returned more calmly to their own dwelling.

2

"This room is simply a clutter," Lottie said. It was a Saturday afternoon and she was seated in her chair: Norris in his. They were drinking after lunch coffee. She frowned. "Perhaps we should weed it out? Though I wouldn't know where to begin." Deirdre came and laid her head on Lottie's lap. The latter's return had been greeted by a fine salvo of barks and shaking of heavy hind quarters.

"In principle," Norris said, "I agree. But piece by piece I find each has associations I wouldn't care to lose. Aunt Rosie's whatnot—that takes me right back to my earliest memories, when I was allowed to look but not to touch. I'm afraid I'm attached to my things—our things."

"Yes," Lottie said. "As I said, I wouldn't know where to begin. It's not any one thing, but there are so many of them."

"We could move to a larger house and spread them about more. Or, conversely, we could move to a small house and have decisions of abandonment forced on us. Some of our pieces are quite valuable. Do you remember how dowdy the rosewood settee seemed when we first fell heirs to it? Now it's high Victoriana."

"I wish the times would hurry up with the dining room set. I'm afraid it's hopelessly twenties Grand Rapids. I remember when it was new! Bless Bess, we've got some good linens to hide it under. Those bulbous legs. I suppose it was a flare-up of the Jacobean taste."

The phone rang. Norris automatically started to rise but Lottie said, "Oh let me. I haven't answered my own phone in an age."

It was Mag Carpenter. "Lottie? I just wanted to say welcome home and how nice I think it is."

"Aren't you kind. Of course I'm really here only for the weekend. A trial flight you might call it."

"Yes, so Maureen told me. But if you can come home for a weekend, surely it means you'll soon be reinstalled in your own castle."

"Castle crowded. I was just saying to Norris that I'd forgotten what a sheer accumulation of stuff we have. I cringe at the thought of getting out the vacuum and the Goddard's wax. I've grown fat and lazy in that comfortable hospital. Spoiled rotten. Now tell me your news."

"Oh, your news—your good news—is about all I know. I just potter on. There's the garden club, where you're sorely missed, and the League, and church. Somehow I fill in the time. I find little shopping trips a great resource. I'm still very much the lonesome widow, but I try to keep my chin up."

"That's very brave of you. I suppose it's the only way. I don't know where I'd be without Norris. Imagine coming back from the hospital to an empty house—it makes me shudder."

"How's that?" Norris said.

"Yes," Mag said, "shudder is the word. I try not to. Now quick, let's get off these depressing topics. As soon as you're back, really truly back, I want to give a little bridge dinner for you. I'll have the Delehanteys too—one of us can take turns sitting out. Frankly, I don't think Maureen is all that crazy about cards."

"Between you, me and the gatepost, she doesn't play as though she were."

Mag laughed. "That's rich. Well, I just wanted to whisper a tiny hello to you. I know you want to get back and visit Norris so I'll sign off."

"Sweet of you to call." And that was over.

"What did Mag want?" Norris asked.

"Nothing," Lottie said, giving Deirdre's ears a tousle. "Just to greet me on my so-called trial flight. I suppose people get used to

(130)

one's being in a hospital, and expect it to become a permanent state. You played bridge several times with Mag: has she gotten any better?"

"Not really, I'm afraid. Or perhaps she has, a little—we gave the Delehanteys a good trouncing. But I had to do all the bidding and play the hands. Mag is one of those players who likes to hold all the aces before she opens her mouth to bid. Luckily Bryan was playing in his usual bull in the china shop style. Now there's a man with a will to win: I'm surprised he's not bankrupt, if that's how he conducts himself in business."

"I've always had the feeling that Bryan is more astute than he seems. It's when he lets down his guard, as in a game of bridge, that he runs hog wild."

"What I don't care for," Norris said, "is the way he's always badgering at those boys. They seem fine lads, if a bit oafish; but then all teen agers tend to be oafs—always falling all over themselves and the furniture and without a word to say."

"Bryan must have had a strict upbringing: parents tend to pass on what they got themselves. And I suppose Bryan views himself as a success in life, ergo, he had the right upbringing."

"Ergo yourself. I think Bryan Delahantey takes himself pretty much as he finds himself—no self-analyst he."

"Lucky man."

"Am I mistaken, Lottie, or is there a fine layer of dust over much of this room?"

"You're not a bit mistaken. Mrs Gompers doesn't have a light hand, whatever she may accomplish with a kitchen floor. Just as well," she added as she regarded various objects of glass and porcelain, especially the shepherd and shepherdess who had come from Meissen. "I wouldn't care for her to be too attentive to some of these things. Still, we're lucky to get anyone these days. Poor Maureen Delahantey harnessed to a floor waxer."

"She has to work off that energy some way, a big woman like that," Norris said, his hand reaching out from old habit toward the afternoon paper. "You won't mind if I take a glance through this?"

"Of course not. Nothing could make me feel more at home." A

beam of sunlight came through the evergreens and into the room, disclosing in its passage the finest of hovering dust.

Meantime, in the Delahantey's living room of gleaming wooden surfaces, Lottie was the topic between Maureen and Biddy. A hellish racket came from above, where the twins were each practicing different music on the instrument of his choice.

"I'm of two minds," Maureen said to the crocheting Biddy, "about whether to ring Mary Charlotte up and say, 'Welcome home,' or to leave well enough alonge. It might seem more natural to take it for granted that *of course* she's in her own home, though only for a weekend. I'll bet a nickle she's already dusting, or washing some of her precious ornaments (I'm always in terror the twins are going to break something when we go there). I wouldn't want to interrupt her if she's up to her elbows in soap suds."

"I won't take you up on your bet, because I never gamble," Biddy said. "As you know. But if I were to hazard a guess, it would be that she and Norris are seated in their living room, making plans. After Lottie's stay in the hospital, I should think a nice trip would be in order—a motor tour, or maybe Florida. Does Norris play golf?"

"I don't think so," Maureen said, and giggled. "Maybe she's out like a light on the kitchen linoleum."

"Honestly, Maureen, you'll be the death of me," Biddy said. "Why don't you go ahead and give a ring and see? You've stirred up my curiosity."

"I think what's holding me back is that I don't know where Mag Carpenter figures in this. You saw what a flight and scurry she flew into in the supermarket the other day. You'd think Lottie was her best friend, and they simply are not all that close. Something is going on, even if it's only in Mag's mind. I'm as certain of that as I am that I'm sitting here." She wriggled her rump in her chair. A volley of trumpet riffs came down the stairs. "I've told those boys not to play that cheap music in this house. Bryan hates it, and so do I. Did you know they want to form a group and play rock and roll music? It's that Nick who's behind it. I understand he has a set of drums. I don't know what their father will say about *that*; except it will be plenty."

"As for Mag Carpenter," Biddy said, "I say, see no evil, speak no evil."

"Heavens, you don't imagine I'd breathe a word to Lottie? Even if I knew something to breathe."

"I was merely expressing my philosophy about situations," Biddy said. "I remember when I was a girl, there was an entanglement that involved the people next door—the husband—and a couple across the street—the wife. Mother said, 'I don't see or know a thing. I'm deaf dumb and blind. It's all invisible to me.' She went right on being friendly with both houses; until the divorces, that is. Then they all moved away. It was a great shame, due to the children, that is. I wonder what ever became of them all? Children of divorced parents seldom turn out well. They tend to go off on their own and get into trouble. I'm grateful that I was never a step-parent."

"No, I wouldn't care to have the bringing up of children who weren't my own. I'd never feel sure I was being fair, being just. There are things you can overlook in your own child that would grate in a step-child. I can see that. I think I *will* give Mary Charlotte Taylor a ring. I don't know why I'm making such a production of it."

She advanced upon a white princess phone and dialed. "Hello? Is that you Norris? Maureen Delahantey here. How is every little thing? I really called up to say a word of greeting to Lottie. Oh. I see. Well tell her not to bother to call back, I just wanted to say hello and wish her a happy welcome home. Do you know yet when she'll be home for good? I see. Still, it can't be far off. Biddy sends her best too. Now take good care of her and we'll expect you both here for dinner and cards in the very near future. Though we needn't play cards if Lottie doesn't feel up to it—I imagine there'll be a little period of adjustment after the hurley-burley of the hospital. Tomorrow is Sunday—if you two feel like coming by for a cup of tea, it would be lovely. See what Lottie says. We won't expect you, just come by if you both feel like getting out of the house. Goodbye for now." She hung up and said to Biddy, "She was taking a nap."

"Perhaps," Biddy said, "you were nearer the truth than you knew about the kitchen floor. Poor woman, I hope she hasn't already taken a false step."

"I don't think she can," Maureen said. "They give them something

(133)

that makes them violently ill if they take a drink. I forget—it's a word like Abuse."

"I can't for the life of me," Biddy said, "guess what made me start on a black afghan. Who will ever want it? I think I'll run a maroon border around it. A nice deep maroon border. That will perk it up."

Back at the Taylor's, Lottie said, "I thought I heard the phone ring while I was dozing."

"It was Maureen," Norris said. "She felicitates you upon your return."

"Thoughtful."

"And said something about dropping by their way tomorrow for a cup of tea if you felt up to it. No need to call."

"I don't. Or is that rude? Of course I'll give her a ring and thank her for the invitation. She'll understand that my first weekend I want to spend here, in my own house. Or would it look funny if we don't go? I don't want people thinking I'm too enfeebled to down a cup of tea."

"If you leave it up to me," Norris said, "I'm not in much of a mood for Bryan Delahantey and his winning ways. The night I played bridge there with Mag Carpenter he told some incredibly off-color stories."

"What were they?"

"I have no memory for dirty jokes, except that they all had to do with defecation. No. I do remember one. It seems an Indian checked into the Palmer House in Chicago and was given a room that shared its bathroom with the room next door. In the morning the chambermaid found the occupant of the adjoining room on the bathroom floor with his throat cut. When asked why he did it, the Indian said, 'Ugh. White man shit in Indian's spring.'"

Lottie snickered. "Bryan is a perennial school boy."

"I don't think Mag cared too much for them, but Maureen laughed her head off, and she must have heard them a hundred times."

"Where was Biddy during all this?"

"Biddy had retired before the hot stuff set in. I don't think Bryan would dare get off one of his good ones in front of his mother."

There was a pause. Lottie drummed her fingers on the arm of her chair, got up, put on some lamps, sat down again and resumed her drumming. "I knew this would happen," she said. "Comes the cocktail hour and I'm dying for a drink like the devil wants souls. Don't worry, I'm not going to have one and make myself sick unto death. But I'll tell you this: I can *hear* the vodka in that kitchen cupboard."

"I don't believe there is any vodka there. You finished it on that last evening . . . "

"And started in on the whiskey. I remember it all, except the falling downstairs part."

"And since I knew you were on the wagon, I haven't replenished the supply. Don't care for it myself. Though I suppose we should stock it for guests."

"Norris?"

"Yes?"

"Please do me a favor. Go mix yourself a pre-dinner drink, and come and drink in here with me."

"I'm not sure I feel like one this evening. I regard alcohol as more of a nightcap."

"Do it for me. It's something I've got to face, and I want to start facing it right now. It's not much to ask."

"No," Norris said, "it isn't." He left the room and returned shortly with a weak scotch and water in a tall glass. No ice—he was a bit of an Anglophile. He took a sip and said, "You're sure, Lottie, that I'm not tormenting you needlessly?"

"No, you're not tormenting me a bit. The seizure, or compulsion, or whatever it was, has passed off. It seems quite natural to see you sitting in your easy chair, having a cocktail hour drink. It was such a funny feeling, like a fit."

"Just don't let the habit grow on me," Norris said.

"Fat chance, with a living reproach in the house. Now I'm going to go heat the broiler for the chops." In the doorway she stopped and turned. "Norris?"

"Yes?"

"Let's go to bed early tonight."

"That," Norris said, "we will certainly do."

(135)

"How was it?" Mrs Brice said. "Tell all."

"It was grand," Lottie said. "I lolled about my own house and reveled in it. On Sunday we went for a drive, and dropped in on some friends for a cup of tea—the Delahanteys. All very pleasant and natural. You met them here once."

"Yes, I remember them well. A large younger woman and an elderly lady, very spry for her years."

"That was Biddy, Maureen's mother-in-law. She's rather a caution. On Sunday she got started on a rambling story about some ne'er-do-well drunkard in her family and his hideous end. Maureen had her work cut out for her getting her off the subject. And Biddy, innocent as the day is long, hadn't a glimmer that it was seeing me that had made the association in her mind. Sometimes I think she is beginning to get a *bit* feeble."

"How trying for you."

"Not really. I have to learn to expect these things and take them as they come. I look on it as good practice. Soon I'll be back out there among the bottles and the boozers and I have to build up strength to fact it. Or them. But let's not talk about me and my peccadillos. Tell me what happened while I was away. How's Mrs Judson?"

Mrs Brice looked all around the almost deserted sun room (Bertha was at the phonograph, shuffling) before she spoke in a lowered voice. "Quite strange. Saturday she was knotting a belt in crafts when she suddenly muttered something, got up and almost ran from the room. She came back shortly, then repeated the whole thing. In fact, she did it several times. I tried to engage her in conversation yesterday, but she was very short with me. Just sitting down for a while, then shooting off and coming back to sit somewhere else."

"I noticed on Friday that she seemed quite manic—manic and angry."

"I wonder," Mrs Brice said, "if it isn't to do with her medication. You remember how clammed-up she was when she arrived here. I suspect they're giving her something to make her more active, to open up and talk about what's eating her."

Mrs Judson entered the room, glared at the pair, started to go to a chair then changed her mind and joined them. "We were discussing Mrs Taylor's—Lottie's—weekend at home. She had a grand time, you'll be pleased to hear."

"That's the greatest news since Lifebuoy soap. If she can go home for a weekend why can't I? She's not any crazier than I am. I mean, I'm not any crazier than she is. Somebody around here is talking about me, and I intend to get to the bottom of it."

"I'll talk about you if you want," Bertha said, coming up to them. "Mrs Judson has delusions, that's what I'll say."

"Oh you," Mrs Judson said, "who would pay any mind to what you said?"

"OK, so I won't talk about you," Bertha said. "Did you get to knock back a few over the weekend?" she asked Lottie.

"No, Bertha, I didn't."

"I'll bet you wanted to all right, but you take that stuff that makes you puke if you do."

"Right on both counts, Bertha. Now let me ask you a question: why do you persist in trying to create bad feelings in the other patients? It doesn't help them, and it makes them dislike you."

"Aw," Bertha said, "can't you take a joke? Everybody's so serious here. I like to kid around a little."

"You're ignoring me," Mrs Judson said in an angry tone. "Deliberately ignoring me."

"Heavens," Lottie said, "what a welcome back."

"Why don't we all have some coffee?" Mrs Brice said brightly.

"Not me," Mrs Judson said. "They put something in it—saltpeter, I suspect. I don't want a lot of chemicals interfering with my natural functions."

"I agree," Lottie said, "that it tastes as though something other than coffee went into it. But I can say that drinking it has not interfered with any of my functions."

"That's what you say," Mrs Judson said.

"Mr Brice says it tastes like old boots," Mrs Brice said.

(137)

"I wouldn't drink it if you paid me," Bertha said.

"You drink up all the soda pop in the ice box," Mrs Judson said to her. "Last night I wanted a ginger ale and there wasn't any left. That's your work."

"Nuts to you," Bertha said, and returned to the phonograph.

Enter Mr Mulwin. "Well, well, well," he said, "or three holes in the ground. Look who's back. How was home sweet home?"

"It was just fine," Lottie said. "I had a delightful two days. You seem in good spirits."

"A lot better than some," Mr Mulwin said.

"Oh," Mrs Judson said, "I'm not going to stand here and be talked about like that." She left the room.

"My gracious," Mrs Brice said. "It's almost impossible not to offend her."

"And when she arrived here," Lottie said, "she was such a sympathetic, mousey little woman."

"Seemed afraid of her own shadow," Mrs Brice said.

"Well," Mr Mulwin said, "that's what they put us in here for: to turn your personality inside out and upside down. I'm just afraid they'll turn me into such a sunny Jim that I won't be able to run my business when I get back home."

"You'll be glad enough to find yourself back in harness," Lottie said. "There's no stopping an old fire-horse like you."

"I believe I'm some years younger than you are, Mrs Taylor," Mr Mulwin said. "What's with this old fire-horse?"

"I intend it as a compliment, but if the remark offends I'll withdraw it."

"How touchy everyone seems this morning," Mrs Brice said. "I wonder if I'll be next to have my toes trod on?" Mr Mulwin feigned stepping on her feet. "Please, nothing physical: I don't like to be touched. That's why I never cared for ballroom dancing. Having some boy's hand planted in the middle of my back. Ugh."

"I loved dancing class," Lottie said. "And if I do say so myself, I was quite a good dancer. A boy I used to date in my girlhood and I were singled out for the waltz." She hummed a few strains of "The Blue Danube." "But Norris doesn't know his left foot from his right, so that was the end of that."

"I'd ask you for a dance," Mr Mulwin said, "but this be-bop rock and roll hooey Bertha plays isn't my style. Ethel and I like to go out dancing. Or we used to. Maybe we will again. It's good exercise and takes your mind off things." He looked over at the pile of records beside the phonograph. "I'll bet there isn't a fox trot in the bunch. Not that my rhumba is all that bad."

"Why you young dancing thing," Lottie said. She did a waltz spin on one foot and dipped. "It takes me back, it takes me back!"

4

"Norris?" Mag said.

"Yes, kitten?"

"What's to become of us?"

"I thought," Norris said, "we'd talked that all out. Nothing is what's going to become of us. It's no good digging that field over again, Mag. We've enjoyed ourselves: isn't that enough? Because I'm afraid it's going to have to be."

"I wish it was I who had died and not Bartram."

"I'm glad you didn't. Bartram was a good fellow, but we wouldn't have hit it off the way you and I have."

"Oh, you tease. You see, Bartram and I were like a pair of old shoes. So when he was taken, it wasn't as though it had happened in the first flush of our romance. And it was a romance. Besides, with his heart, we'd had warnings, so it wasn't the shock it might have been."

"Sometimes I feel like rather an old rooster for these carryings on."

"But not while we're making love?" Mag said.

"No, not then. Not then at all."

"How does that Cole Porter song go? ' . . . a slap and a tickle is all that the fickle male ever has in his head.'"

"Where in Goshen did you pick that up?"

"It was in a musical comedy Bartram and I once saw in New York. I have quite a good memory, though I forget the name of the show.

Sophie Tucker sang it, and Mary Martin was in the cast. She sang, 'My Heart Belongs to Daddy.'"

"I am in no sense musical," Norris said, "but even I remember that one. It was quite a hit."

"I told you I have a good memory—shall I sing it for you? The Mary Martin song, I mean?" And scarcely without pausing she sang through the verses and chorus of "My Heart Belongs to Daddy." When she finished, she reached across the bed and twitched away the towel with which Noris had covered himself.

"Hey," Norris said, hastily pulling up the top sheet.

"Mr Shy and Modest. You don't hide before, why should you afterward? I like to look at you."

"It's the way I am," Norris said. "You make me self-conscious."

"If you'd let me, I bet I could get you to do it twice to me."

"No. You're not going to try. What's gotten into you, baby?"

"I believe it's called lust. Or if you prefer a more refined word, desire. Yes, it's desire. You ought to feel flattered."   .

"I'm more alarmed than flattered," Norris said, not sounding particularly scared. "Act your age."

"That's just what I'm doing, acting my age, which is about that of Mount Etna."

"Mount Etna sometimes becomes dormant."

"Not right now." They tussled on the bed, but Norris would not give in.

"I'm going to take a shower," he said, "and then be sneaking on my way."

"Let me wash your back."

"Okey-dokey said his highness, but no funny business."

Chapter IX

1

"And that's enough about me and my little vacation," Lottie said. "It was pretty much a complete success."

"It was indeed," Norris said.

"Lucky you," Mrs Judson said with her new sarcasm.

"Perhaps in the near future," Sam Judson said, "you'll have a weekend home yourself. I know I look forward to it. We can take some nice drives too. And have a dinner at the Steak Pit."

"A likely story," Mrs Judson said, "with all the things they say about me behind my back. Somebody went through my drawers again. I wish I knew what they were looking for. I have nothing to hide."

The nurse seated in the corner spoke up. "I was looking for the nail scissors. You were the last to have them, and when I asked you for them, you said first that you'd returned them, which you hadn't, and then that you had mislaid them."

"I wanted to keep them a little longer. So I could do my nails in the sun room where the light is better. Good heavens, I can be trusted with a little pair of nail scissors. What do you think I was going to do—try to cut Mr Mulwin's throat?"

"Good grief," Mr Mulwin said, "leave me out of it. You've no call to have a grudge against me."

"I was just using you as an example: yours was the first name that came to mind."

"In leaving you alone with the scissors," Dr Kearney said, "the nurse was evincing trust in you."

"Thank you, doctor," the nurse said. Earlier that afternoon, the head nurse had given her holy hell.

"I *did* give them back," Mrs Judson said. "Don't I deserve any credit for that? I could have thrown them out and pretended I didn't know a thing about it."

"Of course," Dr Kearney said, "but you can also see, I'm sure, how your previous prevarication creates a certain distrust."

"I'm as trustworthy as any one in this room," Mrs Judson said. "More than most, if you really went into it."

"I hate to tattle," Mrs Brice said, "but this afternoon I came unexpectedly into our room and Mrs Judson was just closing a drawer of my dresser. It was the drawer where I keep my stockings and underclothing."

"That was where I hid the scissors," Mrs Judson said, "so I could use them later. I didn't take any of your old things."

"Wild," Bertha said.

"I didn't accuse you of taking anything," Mrs Brice said firmly. "But I'd prefer you didn't go into my drawers. It's about the only privacy I have. Any of us have."

"Yeah," Mr Mulwin said, "don't come mousing around my room and rummaging in the drawers. If you don't mind."

"Why?" Lottie asked in a bantering tone. "Have you something to hide?"

"Step out into the corridor," Mr Mulwin said, "and I'll show you what I've got to hide."

"That will be enough of that," Mrs Mulwin said.

"You see?" Mrs Judson said to her husband. "Now they're talking filthy."

"Ethel," Sam Judson said, "I hate to say this, but for the past week you haven't been yourself. I wish you could figure out what's getting at you and tell us. Or tell Dr Kearney in your private consultation. No one changes so rapidly without a reason."

"I think that's true, Mrs Judson," Mrs Brice said. "Something is making you behave out of character."

"Suppressed rage," Bertha said, "and plenty of it."

"*Oh you*," Mrs Judson hissed. She was trembling. An awkward silence fell on the group. Mrs Judson got up and marched from the room, banging the door. The nurse followed her. They shortly returned and Mrs Judson resumed her seat. She laced her fingers in her lap and stared down at them stolidly.

Mr Brice cleared his throat. "I want to say," he said, "how pleased I am with the progress Fanny—Mrs Brice—has made. I think she's earned a weekend visit home herself. Or at least an evening out and dinner in a restaurant with me, her husband."

"How do the others feel about it?" Dr Kearney queried.

"I've got nothing against it," Mr Mulwin said.

Mrs Mulwin spoke up. "Mrs Brice seems utterly changed from when I first met her. All for the better, I mean. She takes a real part in these sessions and is more confident and out-going."

"How do you feel about it, Fanny?" Lottie asked. "You're the one who knows best."

"I don't know," Mrs Brice said. "I want to be all well and home again, and yet when I think about it, it makes me nervous. A little nervous, a little apprehensive."

"Fear of change," said the oracular Bertha.

"I don't know what associations seeing my home might stir up," Mrs Brice said. "Maybe the gains I've made are only on top, like cat's ice. I might break through and plunge back into my old withdrawn depression. On the other hand, I must confess that I envied Lottie when I heard she was going to have her weekend."

"One way to find out," Dr Kearney said, "would be to take the bull by the horns and risk a visit to what I'm sure is your very pleasant home."

"Yes," Mrs Brice said, "it is pleasant."

"We look forward to a visit home from our daughter," Bertha's mother said.

"Yes," her husband agreed.

"A whiff of freedom makes the whole world kin," Mrs Brice said.

"I'm not ready yet," Bertha said firmly. "I'll let you know when I am."

"Big of you," Mrs Judson said.

"Why Ethel," Sam Judson said.

"Mrs Judson," Lottie said, "I wish you would tell me one thing that I have done to offend you. Or anyone else here, for that matter."

"How could *you* offend me?" Mrs Judson said. "I'm above that."

"And yet you behave toward me as though I had. I'm not trying to provoke you—I think you'll feel better if you get some of what's bothering you off your chest."

"I'll thank you to leave my chest out of it."

"Very well," Lottie said, "I've tried."

"You were going along great guns," Mrs Brice said. "Don't you remember the day you and Miss Pride and I worked over the moccasins together? You hadn't much confidence, and now you're into belt knotting, which is much more difficult."

"Stupid belt," Mrs Judson said. "Idiot moccasins. Horrible hospital: there's nothing wrong with me: I want to go home."

"Who doesn't?" Mr Mulwin said. "I went through a period when I couldn't see any reason why I should be here. Now I can see it was an important step. I'd gotten so I was driving myself so hard I couldn't slow up. I couldn't see that I needed to slow up. Mrs Mulwin saw it, but I didn't. Shock therapy helped me, maybe it would help you. It breaks the pattern. Sure takes it out of you too, I must say. I'm still pooped."

"They wouldn't dare!" Mrs Judson screamed.

"You're alarming my wife needlessly," Sam Judson said. "I don't mean on purpose, but my wife's course of treatment is up to her doctor, not an uninformed layman who is a patient himself."

"What I'd like to know," Mrs Judson said to Lottie, "is the kind of things you and that Mrs Brice say about me when you're both

(144)

muttering away in the sun room."

"Nothing unkind, I assure you," Lottie said. "I did observe to Mrs Brice that you seemed to have become overwrought. That was the extent of it."

"You see?" Mrs Judson said. "They do talk about me. No wonder I'm overwrought. I lead a very private personal life and don't need any intruders in it, thank you. Even if I did take things when I was a little girl, that was just childishness. And after they punished me, I never did it anymore."

"After who punished you?" Norris asked quietly.

"My mother, with a strap." Mrs Judson was racked by a sob. "It wasn't such an awful thing for a little child to do."

"I remember once," Mrs Brice said, "I wanted some candy so badly, and I knew I wouldn't be allowed to have it. So I went into my mother's purse and got some change and bought my candy. Then I was terrified I'd be found out—so terrified I never did it again. Not that I wasn't tempted."

"You never told me that, mother. Remember the time the boy . . ."

"No, let's not remember that. I only want to remember the good things about our boy."

"There weren't many that were at all bad," Mr Brice said.

"No," his wife agreed, "there weren't."

"What was it you took?" Bertha asked Mrs Judson.

"Money. Just a little and just a few times."

"What did you want it for?"

"To buy Nancy Drew mystery stories. I pretended I borrowed them from a girl friend. Then my mother said I ought to return them, so I had to give them away to get out of it. It was awful—even my favorite, *At the Sign of the Twisted Candles*."

"If you were old enough to read Nancy Drew," Bertha said, "you weren't all that little a child. I thought you meant you were about five or six."

"She beat me and beat me and then she said she was going to put me in a home."

"And here you are," Norris said.

(145)

"I imagine," Lottie said, "that you feel it's your mother who's put you here, and that's what makes you so resentful of the hospital. It's touched on an old nerve."

"I don't steal things now," Mrs Judson said. "I never took anything after that that didn't belong to me. I'm not a thief, am I Sam?"

"Of course not dear, you're as honest as the day is long."

"You see?" Mrs Judson said to the nurse.

"I'm sure the nurse never meant to accuse you of theft," Dr Kearney said, "but simply of practicing a small deception."

"You mean I'm a liar," Mrs Judson said.

"I think we all are," Norris said, "when the small occasion arises. Wanting to trim your nails in the sun room doesn't strike me as a major crime."

"I don't steal and I don't tell lies," Mrs Judson said. "That's that."

"I believe you on both scores," Norris said. "I wish I could say the same for myself. I'm always asking my secretary to tell some bore or other that I'm out or tied up. That's lying. I don't think I could get through a business day without a few small falsehoods. They grease the wheels."

"Oh, if that's what you mean by *lying*," Mr Mulwin said.

"It's plain to see," Mrs Brice said, "that the Second Coming has not yet occurred."

"Do you think it will occur?" Dr Kearney asked, smiling.

"I do indeed. It's a tenet of our church. I don't believe in giving mere lip-service to my faith."

"Personally," Bertha said, "I think it's an open question. And I don't know what all this fuss about taking a little money is all about. I knew kids in college who would rip off somebody's phonograph and pawn it to buy dope."

"Why Bertha," her mother said, "I had no idea the university was like that. I hope you never . . ."

"No," Bertha said, "I never. But I might have if I hadn't had such a good allowance."

"What's past is past," Bertha's father said. "We must cast our eyes to the future."

"When I was a boy," Mr Mulwin said, "I got to be quite an

accomplished shop-lifter. I'd work with one of the guys in my gang. He'd distract the clerk and I, bold as brass, would pick up some little thing. Finally we got careless and the manager of Woolworth's almost cornered me. Boy, did I hoof it! Never set foot in that store again, even when I was grown up. It taught me a lesson: I teach all my clerks to keep their eyes skinned when a couple of kids come into the store and split up. I tell them, ask, 'Do you want something, boys?' And if they don't answer up, ask them not to hang around. Not that it's just kids. I personally caught a lady trying to slip a big box of imported soap into her handbag. I took her into the back of the store and put the fear of God into her—one of our best charge customers, would you believe it."

"At this point," Lottie said, "I'll believe about anything."

"Now I can see," Mr Mulwin went on, "I should have gotten in touch with her husband. She was sick. Belonged here. There's a word for it."

"Kleptomania," Norris said.

"Yes, that's the one. Kleptomania. She was the genuine article."

"I am not a shop-lifter," Mrs Judson said.

"No one said you were," Mr Judson said. "You must stop thinking that any little remark is indirectly meant for you."

"That's the way people talk about you," Mrs Judson said. "They say it about somebody else, then they give you a look."

"I wasn't talking about you," Mr Mulwin said. "And I can't help giving you a look: I'm sitting across the table from you, for Pete's sake."

"A quiet game of bridge," Lottie said, "would be most welcome about now."

"These sessions take it out of you," Mrs Brice said.

"I'm not tired," Mrs Judson said. "I'm fresh as a daisy. I can face up to it and protect myself."

"No one's attacked you," Mr Mulwin said in a lackluster voice.

"When are we going to talk about me?" Bertha asked. "I sure hope I'm not going to be like any of you when I'm your age."

"Go jump in the river," Mrs Judson said.

2

Maureen rapped on the twins' door and went in without waiting for an answer. "A funny thing has happened," she said. "As a matter of fact it isn't funny at all. I went to the bank this morning and drew out some money. I knew just how much I had. Just now I paid the paper boy, and for some reason, I counted my money again. I'm short five dollars, and I know I didn't lose it. Did either of you go in my purse and take five dollars? I want the truth."

Patrick was sitting on his side of the desk, staring, while Michael across from him had a notebook open. Both boys shook their heads, without saying a word.

"I'm going to get to the bottom of this," Maureen said. "I want you both to stand up and turn out your pockets. Put everything in them on the desk."

"I did not," Michael said, "take anything out of your purse."

"Do as I say," Maureen said.

Slowly the boys got to their feet and emptied their pockets. Change, chewing gum, keys (Michael's were on a lucky rabbit's foot chain), handkerchiefs, and, in Patrick's case, a packet of condoms. Maureen stared at the latter and flushed. "Where did you get the money for those?" she said.

"Out of my allowance." The packet had a dog-eared look and clearly had not been bought that day.

"Don't ever let me see that again," Maureen said. "Now I want you to turn your pockets right inside out. The hip pockets, too."

The boys did so. No five dollar bill emerged.

"I just don't know," Maureen said. "If I've done you an injustice, I apologize." She left the room.

Michael stared at Patrick until the other's gaze wavered and he looked away. "You took it. I *know* I didn't, so you must have." Patrick didn't answer. "You really are going to get in dutch one of these days. Now Mom will start thinking Biddy's getting old and starting to take things. Old people get like that."

"Maybe she did," Patrick said.

"Bullshit. Where'd you hide it?

"In my shoe."

"You realize you're stark raving crazy don't you? Mom has a photographic memory."

"Well," Patrick said reasonably, "I didn't think she'd miss it. The purse was lying there so I looked inside and the wallet was stuffed with money. I took it before I knew I'd done it."

"I've seen it coming for a long time and now I know it: you're insane. They'll lock you up with Mrs Taylor and the rest of the nuts."

"Since when are you such a saint? What about the time Dad caught you going through his jacket?"

"Come on: I was just a little kid then. I didn't know any better."

"You weren't too little to get your ass whacked good."

"Stop acting like I'm going to squeal on you: you know I won't. What did you want the money for, anyway? Five dollars!"

"I wanted to buy some grass off of Pete."

"Oh wow. I thought you didn't even like it. You told me you didn't trust it—your very words. I was the one who got the good high."

"I thought it over and decided I wanted to give it a second chance. It was kind of interesting."

"Pete told me he didn't have any more," Michael said. "The big liar."

"He didn't. Then his brother at college's contact told him about a contact here, in the city, and his brother passed the word along to Pete. He's going to get an ounce, but first he has to get the money together, so four of us are chipping in. See? Don't worry, you'll get some of it."

"How come you didn't tell me about it? We could have gotten it together out of our allowances. I need a new notebook and stuff. I could ask Dad for money for that. Or Mom. Or I could have, before this happened. You dope."

Patrick shuddered. "Boy, I'll never do that again," he said fervently. "Actually, I was sitting here trying to think of a way to put it back before Mom noticed."

Dinner that night was a gloomy occasion. Bryan finally said, "What's on your mind, Maureen? You act like you're off in another world."

Maureen explained about the missing bill and said, "The teller may accidentally have short changed me, only I'm so certain I counted it myself and it came out right."

"How did you find you were short?" Bryan asked.

"It was after I paid the paper boy. I had to ask him if he could change a five, which he did in rather a surly way, and then when I put my purse down, I thought, 'That's funny, I thought I had *two* fives.' So I counted up what I had and it didn't come out right. And I haven't been to the store or anything."

Bryan put down his fork and looked from one boy to the other. "No, no," Maureen said. "I've been into it with the twins. Neither of them took it. I don't know why I suspected them. Still, boys will be boys and at the time it seemed a likely explanation."

"Of course they didn't take it," Biddy said, "my chicks aren't like that."

"They'd better not be," Bryan said threateningly. "Were they new bills? They may have stuck together and you gave him them by mistake."

"That's a thought, though I've never done that before. I'm going to call him up and ask him. What's the paper boy's name?"

Michael told her, and what street the family lived on. Maureen left the room and returned a few minutes later. "He says I didn't, but I suppose if I did, it would seem like manna from Heaven to him. He was quite offended. I had to explain that I wasn't accusing him of taking it, only that I might have made a mistake."

"Little twerp," Bryan said. "You want me to speak to him?"

"What good would that do?" Maureen said. "He'd only deny it again. Next thing you know the boy's father would be over here, accusing us of accusing his son of God knows what and there'd be no end to it."

"These mysterious things happen," Biddy said. "It's like the keys to the old Reo. Father was going out one day and forgot something—or rather, remembered something—at the last moment. He

(150)

put the keys down on the drainboard in the kitchen and went out of the room and when he came back, they were gone. It was mystery that went unsolved. Mother's theory was that he had put them some place else, a suggestion that made him quite ferocious. It was always my belief that one of my brothers took them, in a spirit of mischief and vengeance, and threw them away. I was devoted to my brothers, but father was strict and when one of them thought he'd been punished unjustly he would often do quite unusual things. Ben, especially. Once he put all the mail in the fire, just like that. But these keys to the Reo. It got so that if they were alluded to Father would turn red as a beet, so the subject was quietly allowed to drop."

"What's a Reo?" Michael asked.

"It was a brand of automobile," Biddy said. "We had one of the first ones in town."

"I can't say I care for this business of money disappearing," Bryan said.

"No more do I," Maureen said. "But I'm not going to let it prey on my mind."

"Dad," Patrick said, "can we go uptown for a little while after supper?"

"No, you can't," Bryan said. "I've seen that gang that hangs around the Candy Kitchen and I don't think much of them. You stay home and study. Your marks are a long way from what they might be."

"They're just guys from school," Michael said.

"Don't say 'guys' dear," Biddy said. "Say, 'boys'."

"Boys," Michael said.

"Boys or guys or young thugs, this is a weeknight and you're both staying home," Bryan said. "Is that clear?"

"Yes, Dad," Patrick said. The five dollar bill was burning a hole in his shoe. "Only I need some notebook paper."

"Borrow it from Michael. You can buy some tomorrow."

"You said we didn't have to buy school supplies out of our allowances," Patrick said.

"Oh, that's the way it is," Bryan said. "Here," and he gave him two dollars. "That ought to buy enough paper to choke a horse."

"I use up as much notebook paper as he does," Michael said. "We do the same amount of homework."

"Two dollars ought to buy enough paper for you both. I haven't got any more singles on me."

"School supplies are dreadfully expensive nowadays," Maureen said. "I've noticed. I'll give you the money in the morning, Michael. But see you bring back every cent of the change. You boys receive ample allowances."

"When I started school," Biddy said, "I had a slate and a piece of chalk. That was all the supplies we needed. And a little sponge to clean it with. I used to love cleaning my slate and making it all nice and black again."

"Slate isn't black," Patrick said, "it's gray."

"Don't talk fresh to your grandmother," Bryan said.

"Oh I know what he means," Biddy said. "But it is black when it's wet. That black afghan. I wish I'd never started it. Somehow it's like a pall. I can hardly wait to finish it and start putting the red edging on. I hope that will help."

"Why not beflower it?" Maureen asked.

"That's a good thought," Biddy said.

"If you let us go uptown now," Patrick said, "we could get the paper at the Candy Kitchen. They stock school supplies."

Bryan bellowed. "No means no," he said. "Not another word about it."

"I don't see any harm in it myself," Maureen said.

"Please," Bryan said in his deepest tone, like something in an old belltower, "please do not countermand my orders."

And there the matter rested.

3

"Good morning," Mrs Judson said to Lottie.

"It is a nice morning, isn't it," Lottie responded. "Tell me, may I call you Ethel? All this missus-ing seems so formal."

"It's all right with me. Lottie. Somehow I don't see myself calling

Mrs Brice 'Fanny'. She's a little more stand-offish than you are. No rudeness meant, on either side. I feel better today, not so harried from pillar to post. Thought you might like to know."

"I am glad. I went through a dreadful spell myself. But let's not talk about that—as Bertha's father said, we must cast our eyes toward the future."

"I don't know what made me think everybody was out to get me, so to speak. After all, we're all just folks here, stuck in the same mess."

"It makes me happy that you realize Mrs Brice and I weren't ganging up on you behind your back. We aren't like that."

"And that business with the nail scissors," Mrs Judson went on. "That was just childishness."

"I suppose inside each of us a child lingers. I know that I've had quarrels with my husband, Norris, that on my side amounted to little more than tantrums. Right now, in here, it's hard to believe we ever quarrel, though I don't doubt we will again. Human nature."

Mrs Brice joined them. "Isn't anybody going to craft therapy today?"

"I was just telling Lottie," Mrs Judson said, "that I feel better today. Perhaps I will go on knotting that belt."

"That is good news," Mrs Brice said.

"What to paint, what to paint," Lottie said as they strolled along the corridor. "I think I'd like to try a portrait—would you pose for me, Ethel?"

"I don't know. I mean, I'd like to, but I'm afraid I'm still too restless. Don't you have to sit perfectly still as a mouse when you pose?"

"Well," Lottie said, "it helps."

"Why not ask Bertha?" Mrs Brice said. "Sitting still would be good for her, and she might like the attention."

"You're sure I wouldn't be inviting trouble? Bertha is a quixotic little miss."

"There's that side to it, too," Mrs Brice said.

"And here are my champion workers," Miss Pride said as the three entered the craft therapy room. "Going to go on with your belt, Mrs

(153)

Judson?" she added in a bright tone.

Bertha was already there, deep in the clay. She frowned heavily, lest anyone speak to her.

"I started it," Mrs Judson said, "so I might as well finish it. I'm certainly not going to wear the ugly thing, but I brought my children up to complete their undertakings, so I suppose I must live up to my own advice."

"I don't think it's going to be ugly," Mrs Brice said, moving to her own belt knotting board. "The colors are very pretty—so harmonious. I see it worn with a neutral colored frock."

"Damn," Bertha said calmly, as she gouged an eye in her lump of clay. "Before you chatterers arrived a person could concentrate."

"Try to adapt, dear," Lottie said. "You can't expect us to give up all converse for the sake of one."

"I don't expect it," Bertha said, "but I sure would like it."

"Ah, is it safe for an unaccompanied male in here?" Mr Mulwin entered. "Miss Pride, good morning to you. You're looking pert as all get out."

"Oh Mr Mulwin." Miss Pride, who was given to blushing, blushed.

"Tell me, Miss Pride," Lottie said, as she got out her brushes and other gear, "how did you happen to take up this line of work?"

Miss Pride thought. "There were a number of reasons. I studied sociology in college, and found I was interested in people. I like working with them. Then I've always liked crafts, since my days at summer camp. And then, too, there was the consideration of earning a living."

"That can be done in a number of ways," Mr Mulwin said.

"I suggest," Miss Pride said to Mrs Judson, "that you pull the knots tighter. Otherwise, the finished belt will be stretchy and hang loose."

"Do you mean I should unknot all I've done and start over? That's too disheartening."

"No, no," Miss Pride said, "that won't be necessary. Here, let me demonstrate what I mean."

"I'm afraid it's going to turn out like those floppy moccasins," Mrs

(154)

Judson said.

"You see? You want to maintain an even tension in your knotting."

"I'm too erratic for that," Mrs Judson said, "but I'll try."

"Making another caricature of me, Bertha?" Mr Mulwin asked.

"Don't be so egotistical," Bertha said. "I have other things on my mind than your big head."

"Good," Mr Mulwin said, "good, good, good."

"Perhaps," Lottie said, "you, Mr Mulwin, are just the victim I'm looking for. Could I persuade you to sit for me? I'd like to try my hand at a portrait. I promise nothing about the results, but I won't *deliberately* insult you."

"Well, I was going to play gin rummy with that new guy—what's his name?"

"Mr Carson," Mrs Brice said, knotting away at a great rate. "He's a merchandizing executive. Very interesting."

"But he seems to have been called away by his shrink, so, why not? I'm certainly not getting mixed up with any moccasins. Shall I sit here? Can I talk? In the event that anything to say occurs to me."

"Yes," Lottie said, "sit right there. Talk all you want—I'm just going to rough you in in charcoal."

"Yetch," Mr Mulwin said, "to borrow a Berthaism."

"Lay off," Bertha said. "I'm in a bad mood."

"OK. You seem in better spirits, Mrs Judson, if I may say so."

"I am. Only please don't tease me. I'm trying to concentrate on these knots."

"Don't concentrate too hard," Mrs Brice said. "Let your fingers do the work. You'll find they've picked up the rhythm and do it natur-ally, of themselves."

"Mine don't seem to," Mrs Judson said. "I suppose it's my lack of self-confidence. How you do fly along at yours."

"And I'm not thinking about it a bit," Mrs Brice said. "I don't think about it on purpose. Have faith in your fingers, that's my advice."

"I'll try."

"Oh fuck," Bertha said. She violently smeared down the bust which she had begun to model. Then she left the room.

(155)

"I do wish Bertha would mind her mouth," Mrs Judson said.

"Pay it no mind," Lottie said. "They say it's an old Anglo-Saxon word, even if it does make me jump. But she only does it to shock—don't give her the satisfaction."

"I'll try," Mrs Judson said. "In fact, it doesn't bother me quite so much as it did. When she opens her mouth, I expect the worst to come out."

"You know, Mr Mulwin," Lottie said, "you have a most interesting head."

"You wouldn't be flirting with me, by any chance?" Mr Mulwin asked.

"By no manner of means," Lottie said.

"Well, all you lovely ladies locked up in here with us few men, I sometimes wonder how safe we are. I know I'd lock my door at night, only it doesn't have a key."

"I'm inclined to say, 'Act your age, Mr Mulwin,' only I suspect that that is what your are doing."

"Playing the old goat? Why don't you call me Greg? Everybody in my business does. Except the clerks, of course. That is, if I may call you Lottie, Mrs Taylor."

"Please do, Greg."

"And what about you, Mrs Brice?" Greg Mulwin went on. Lottie had swiftly sketched in a large head which bore some resemblance to the sitter.

"I may have bitten off more than I can chew," Lottie said.

"If it's all right with you, I'd prefer it if you went on calling me Mrs Brice. Scarcely anyone calls me Fanny, so I'm not used to it. Except Mr Brice, and he usually calls me Mother." Mrs Brice gave one of her rare chuckles. "And I don't think I'm *quite* old enough to be *your* mother, younger though you are."

"Not possible," Greg Mulwin said, "no way. Posing is peaceful and relaxing work. Perhaps I'll give up pharmaceuticals and get a job in an art school. May I come to you for a letter of recommendation, Lottie?"

"That you may."

A nurse entered the room. "Isn't Bertha here? Doctor wants to see

(156)

her."

"She was here," Miss Pride said. "But she was dissatisfied with her work and left."

"In fact," Greg Mulwin said, "you might say she shot out of here hell for leather."

"She's not in her room or the sun room," the nurse said, "or the bath."

"Did you look in the kitchenette?" Lottie said. "She's very given to soda pop and can often be found in the vicinity of the refrigerator."

"She's not there," the nurse said. "You know, Miss Pride, you are responsible for the patients who take craft therapy when they're working in here."

"I beg your pardon," Miss Pride said stiffly, "but that is not my understanding of the case. I am a therapist, not a guard."

The nurse left on silent shoes.

"Dollars will get you doughnuts," Mr Mulwin said, "that our Bertha has pulled a flit. I've often noticed that if the attention of the nurse on reception is diverted, it would be easy as cake to walk right out the door."

"She seemed in a mood to do just that," Lottie said.

"Oh dear," Mrs Judson said. "More trouble. I hope she hasn't gone and done something foolish."

Dr Kearney came in. "I understand Bertha was last seen in here. Or rather, leaving here. How did she seem? What was she doing?"

Miss Pride turned pink, and spoke. "She was working on a bust. In clay." She indicated the clay on its stand. "One she started yesterday."

"Yes, yes," Dr Kearney said.

"She seemed quite morose and rather hostile toward the others. Then she suddenly left," Miss Pride finished.

"She used a curse word—the worst one," Mrs Judson put in excitedly, "Messed up her work and stormed out with clay all over her hands. I thought she'd gone to wash."

"It would seen we have trusted Bertha unjustifiably." Dr Kearney gave Miss Pride a look that brought more roses to her cheeks. He turned to leave, then stopped and added, "All grounds privileges are

(157)

suspended until further notice." Then he was gone.

"I knew it," Mrs Judson said. "More trouble."

"I'm not sure I call that fair," Mrs Brice said. "He surely can't think we're all going to run away because of what an overwrought child does. I was so looking forward to my afternoon stroll."

"And it's such a beautiful day," Lottie said. "Where in the world can she run to? She can't have much in the way of money. She borrowed ten cents from me yesterday to make a phone call."

"She won't get far," Mr Mulwin said. "Don't worry, she'll turn up like the proverbial bad penny."

4

It was night. Mag Carpenter was seated at the desk in what had always been called Bartram's study. She was reading through a sheaf of notepaper, a letter she had just finished. Her handwriting was large, blockish, and slightly backhand. In her school days she had drawn little circles over her i's. These lingered in a vestigial way, like little commas lying on their sides.

> *Dearest Norris,*
>
> *How to begin? I sometimes try to have a little chat with you, talk things over, but you are so acute and quick that the subject is soon changed. I'm left feeling I haven't said what I wanted to. Though by no means sure what that is!*
>
> *It's late and I couldn't sleep. Took a pill but it had no effect at all. The doctor said the most I can take is two but I can tell another one won't make a bit of difference. Anyway, I began thinking and thought perhaps I'd write you a letter, one I can give you when next we meet. This way I may be able to say what's on my mind. It's worth a try anyway and what harm can it do? You can read it and tear it up and never allude to it, if that is your wish. I imagine it will be. It seems like your way, dear.*
>
> *What you don't realize—don't know—is how unhappy I*

(158)

am. Not when I'm with you—that isn't what I mean. My days are a kind of hell on earth. Because I miss you—and we don't see each other all that often do we? More because of what the future holds or rather doesn't hold.

Thinking of course of when Lottie is back home. You have been very clear about that but like any woman or person I have my day dreams. Isn't there some way we can go on seeing each other other? Not often—now and then.

I know if you had a job where you traveled it could all work out very easily. Our meeting now and then, I mean.

I feel I must be as truthful with you as I am with myself. I've said repeatedly I wouldn't for worlds want to come between you and Lottie. That is a flat lie. It would be my dream come true if you and she divorced and you married me. Don't misunderstand. I know that won't happen. But when I'm alone that's the way my thoughts turn. I know I could make you happy. I do make you happy, don't I? You do me, but you know that already.

You're so much more wonderful a lover than B. was, though it seems unfair to say it. Sometimes I wish we had never gotten launched on our little affair—then I would never have known. But then I would never have known this wonderful happiness, Norris dear, and I think I can truthfully say I would rather have that and the future (unhappiness) than not to have known you this way. If the Gods gave me a chance to have a clean slate and go back to before, not knowing, I wouldn't take it! Not on your life.

Well, I am rambling on at a great rate. There must be some one thing I want to say to you and it is this. Won't you reconsider? Isn't it possible that we could meet now and then after Lottie is back home? I know it wouldn't be often but I don't ask for that. Oh dear, dearest Norris. Perhaps in the future you will find you miss me and want to see me, too? I can't count on that though. You are so very decisive.

It seems funny—a trait I admire about you is precisely what's making me so unhappy. You funny man. You make

(159)

me laugh so much (when we're together) and then here I am
alone and unhappy. Doesn't make too much sense does it?

Please don't think I'll do anything indiscreet—you know
me better than that.

The nights are long and the days are dull. I shouldn't go
on like this to you—I'm afraid I'll only succeed in frighten-
ing you away.

What a silly billy I am. Don't take anything in this letter
too seriously. Just picture your Mag late at night, feeling
blue, deciding to write you a letter and doing it. They say
there has to be a first time for everything, and this is it for
me. Or you are.

You know I love you and when you make love to me I feel
you love me too. There. I can't speak plainer than that. Can
I? It would fit on a postcard. Perhaps that's what I should
do, copy that sentence on a postcard and send it to you at
your office! Don't frown! I'm only teasing.

See what you make of this letter and then let's talk about
it. Now I'm going back to bed and see if I can't woo
Morpheus. Till next we meet—all my love,

Mag

Mag read this through several times, put it down and went to the
kitchen and made herself a light scotch and water. She came back to
the study and read the letter again. Then she tore it into little pieces
and dropped them in the wastebasket. She sat at the desk a long time,
now and then taking a sip of her drink. Then she got up and went
back to the kitchen. She opened the oven and looked into it, then took
out the racks. She knelt down and put her head tentatively into the
oven. She got up and fetched the kitchen chair and lay down across it
and the oven door, her head within the oven, reached up and turned
on the gas. After a minute she pulled her head out, turned off the gas
and went to the sink and began to vomit. Tears ran down her face as
she turned on the faucet and washed her sickness away. She started

to go upstairs, turned back and replaced the racks in the oven, put the kitchen chair in its usual place and opened the window a crack. She stood in her kitchen and said aloud, "I won't try that again." She put out the light and that in the study, went upstairs, took two more sleeping pills and went to bed.

There really seemed no way out.

Chapter X

1

Bertha was back, and the new patient, Mr Carson, was seated also at the crowded table. His wife, a mousey woman much shorter than he, was sitting a little to one side and behind him.

"I wasn't going anywhere," Bertha said, "when the nurse found me at the bus stop. For one thing, I didn't have the fare. And it's too far to walk out to where we live. And if I had gotten home you'd just have brought me back here anyway," she added to her parents.

"Of course, dear," her mother said.

"That's what you're here for," her father said. "To learn how to control these destructive impulses. I don't mean you did anything especially bad, but it's a set-back in your treatment, running off like that. It makes you seem irresponsible."

"Maybe she wanted a breath of air," Mr Carson said in a kindly voice. Under his jacket sleeves it could be seen that both his wrists were bandaged. "Everyone needs that, once in a way."

"It wasn't a *plan*," Bertha said. "I saw that nurse up by the door wasn't really looking so I just walked past, down the hall and out the door. It wasn't so much that I *thought*, 'I've got to get out of here.' I just seized the opportunity and got."

"I can understand that so well," Lottie said. "That's the way I used to be about drinking. I didn't plan to take a drink or even think of it, I just took one. Down the hatch. Sometimes I was quite surprised to find myself standing there with a glass in my hand."

"That's all behind you," Norris said.

"I don't think we need make such a fuss over Bertha's little slip up," Mrs Brice said. "It's like losing your temper—apologies all round and then best forget it."

"Try telling him that." Bertha indicated Dr Kearney, lounging at the head of the table.

"The question has arisen," Dr Kearney said, "or rather, Bertha's escapade has caused the question to arise, whether this is the best place for her. This is an open ward, and a patient who has been here as long as Bertha is expected, is trusted to live up to the rules. You might say what we have here is a co-operative venture and patients who don't co-operate need some other kind of care, of therapy."

"Oh great," Bertha said. "You see? They're going to ship me off to some sort of hoosegow hospital. Locked wards and all that jazz—not that I've had all that much freedom here."

"Oh come, dear," her mother said. "You yourself said you didn't feel ready for grounds privileges. But I do think Bertha deserves another chance."

"What do you others think?" Dr Kearney sounded bored.

"I think Bertha has improved in every way," Mrs Brice said firmly.

"I'll buy that," Lottie said. "I've grown quite fond of her and think of her as, 'our Bertha'."

"In many ways," Norris said, "Bertha seems to me the patient who has made the greatest progress. She was certainly a most disturbed young woman at the time my wife came here."

"I'm all for giving a person the benefit of the doubt," Mr Carson said. "But my opinion isn't worth much. Since I just got here. My opinion isn't worth much, period, come to think of it."

(164)

Mrs Carson gave a little squeak of protest.

"Mrs Judson?" Dr Kearney said, "haven't you an opinion?"

"Well, it seems to me it's up to you doctors to decide what's for the best. I mean, that's what you're trained for, isn't it? I've nothing against Bertha or her staying here—even if her language isn't always what I'd care to hear. But I can put up with it. I think she only does it to get a rise out of we older women."

"There's never been any strong language used around home," Sam Judson said. "My wife isn't used to it."

"So I'm to be sent to Siberia," Bertha said, "because I cuss a little bit and went for a walk. Big deal."

"What do you think of your own progress, Bertha?" Lottie asked. "Now that we've all had our little say."

Bertha became morose. "How can I tell? I don't stand around watching myself."

"Yes," Lottie persisted, "but how do you feel—how do you seem to yourself."

"Like the same old Bertha. There never was all *that* much the matter with me. Well, I guess on the other hand lying on the hall floor in a coma so everybody had to step over me wasn't exactly normal, or whatever you want to call it. But those were things I couldn't help. I didn't decide to go bonkers—I just kind of slid into a pit."

"And now you've climbed a good way out of it," Lottie said. "Don't you think you should give yourself some credit for your own exertions?"

"It's mostly the dope—the medicine—they give you that does that."

"I don't think you should give all the credit to the medicine," Mrs Brice said. "You could have gone on lying on the floor till the day of doom if you'd a mind to. You're a very determined girl: for good or for bad is for you to decide. I think you've decided pretty much for the good."

"I don't see why you should be nice to me," Bertha said. "I'm never particularly nice to you."

"I don't pay any mind to that. You're just being yourself: and that I can rather admire. A person has to have spunk in this world."

"And Bertha has her fair share of that," Mrs Judson said, lapsing into her mood of a few days previous.

"Without some spunk, you won't get anywhere in life," Mr Mulwin said. "I wish I felt some welling up in me, instead of feeling so damn tired all the time. You stick to your guns, Bertha, don't let them walk all over you."

"Do you want to stay or do you want to go?" Dr Kearney suddenly said to Bertha. "By and large, the choice lies pretty much with you."

"I guess I want to stay. I want to get well and get out of here, like everybody else. Go back to school. Have some fun with people my own age. But why should you believe that?"

"No reason," Dr Kearney said, "if you pull stunts like this running away. You upset some of the patients, you took a lot of the staff away from their work, in general you made a nuisance of yourself. And a center of attention. Do you think that may have had anything to do with it?"

"No," Bertha said with admirable firmness. "I wasn't thinking about being a center, I wasn't thinking about anything, except I was in a bad mood and had an impulse and acted on it. If you let me stay, I'll try to exercise more self-control. That's what you want, isn't it?"

"How long, oh Lord, how long?" Mrs Judson said.

"Until the dreadful journey's done," Mrs Brice said, sotto voce.

"Why, Fanny," Lottie said.

"I think it's a quotation," Mrs Brice said. "I don't mean anything by it."

"This all reminds me of a song," Mr Carson said in his pleasant voice. " 'I'll be hard to handle/ I'll be up to tricks,' I think it went. But I can't trust my memory."

"We want you to be *your*self, Bertha," Dr Kearney said, "not at the mercy of this other self who indulges in moods and impulses that are, as you well know, destructive."

"Isn't that what any of us wants?" Norris said.

"How about if I said I'm sorry and won't do it again?" Bertha said.

"Apologies don't count for much around here," Dr Kearney said. "Lip service."

"He means actions speak louder than words," Mrs Judson said.

"Why don't you shut up?" Bertha said. "I'm sorry. That slipped out. I guess I'm just another lost cause."

"I don't think," Lottie said, "anyone wants you to inhibit yourself. It's more a matter of how you direct your energies. I must say, I think it's hard—a young person with a lot of vim cooped up with us older fuddy-duddies."

"Fuddy-duddy," Mr Carson said, "that about describes it. I couldn't even carry this through to completion." He shot back his cuffs and exhibited his bandages.

"What did you use?" Bertha asked with lively interest, "a razor blade?"

"No. A keen-edged paring knife."

"I threw it out," Mrs Carson said. "I never wanted to see it again."

"It wasn't the knife's fault," Mr Carson said in a reasonable tone. "I woke up in the night—you could hardly say I'd been to sleep— feeling low. So after a while I went down in the kitchen and got it and tried to take my life—to open my veins. But, as usual, I was just making a hash of it so I called my wife and she came down and we wound up here. At least I did: she went home after a while."

"What a piteous story," Mrs Brice said. "How well I know those watches of the night, when you can't sleep, and your thoughts go around in circles, and you feel low."

"I once *threatened* to kill myself," Mrs Judson said. She seemed to preen a little. "Of course now it wouldn't enter my mind. I've as much right to live as the next one."

"Sometimes you talk as though you had more right," Bertha said. "You talk like someone was trying to take it away from you."

"The person who threatens suicide," Sam Judson said, "or makes an unsuccessful attempt, is signaling for help. They have problems they can't handle on their own. I read that."

"That has a familiar ring," Mr Mulwin said. "I read it somewhere too. *Reader's Digest*, I think."

"There must be those," Lottie said, "who only mean to signal, but succeed. A chilling thought."

"They say God's mercy is infinite," Mrs Brice said. "I can't say

(167)

I've had any personal experience of it, but it must mean something if they say it."

"You mean," Mr Mulwin asked, "to each his appointed time?"

"No I don't," Mrs Brice said. "There was no appointed time about what happened to my Thad and his family. It was a stupid, stupid accident. It left me feeling there's no meaning in anything . . . and yet, I don't know. God's will be done, only I can't believe that accident was God's will."

"Of course not," Norris said. "Who would want to believe in a God like that? Much less worship Him. But then, I am not myself a believer."

"Check," Bertha said. "You pays your money and you takes your chance."

"She talks dirty, she runs away and puts everyone in a fuss, and she doesn't believe in God. What next?" Mrs Judson said.

"Lay off," Bertha said. "I have as much right to my opinions as you have."

"I have no opinion," Mrs Judson said. "But I know bad manners when I meet them. Excuse me," she said to Bertha's parents, "but I think your daughter is spoiled."

"I may have indulged Bertha more than I should," Mrs Hartz said, "but she was always a strong natured child and I tried to give her her head. Appearances to the contrary, I don't think I was altogether wrong."

"Yes," Mr Hartz said, "why not give our daughter a rest and talk about yourself? You have some problems of your own, I've noted."

"I'm not sure I like your tone," Sam Judson said.

"Like it or lump it," Bertha said.

"Let's not become acrimonious," Lottie said. "That's not the way in which we can help each other. Mrs Judson will speak up in her own good time, I'm sure of that."

"I thought you were going to call me by my first name?" Mrs Judson said. "Lottie."

"It was just a slip, Ethel."

"Why should a person feeling low make him want to take his life?" Mr Carson asked. "I mean, one person rather than another.

(168)

Everyone must feel low some time or other."

"I certainly do," Norris said. "But I find a good night's sleep usually puts it right."

"A good night's sleep!" Mr Carson exclaimed. "I'm forced to say I don't think you know what it means to feel really low."

"I can usually get to sleep," Bertha said, "and I've been lower than an earthworm's belly. So I don't think sleep has much to do with it."

"I was only speaking for myself," Norris said.

"Since I came here," Mr Carson said, "I haven't felt quite so low. Maybe things will take a turn for the better; though I'm probably mistaken."

"Do you play bridge?" Lottie asked.

Mr Mulwin laughed. "Mrs Taylor and her deck of cards: the universal panacea."

"It is a distraction from oneself, *and* one's troubles," Lottie said. "At least, I find it so."

"I haven't played since college," Mr Carson said. "I'm afraid I'd just hold up the game."

"Oh we're not card sharks," Mrs Brice said. "I'm the rankest kind of amateur, but I enjoy it. It is a diversion. And then there's craft therapy—you'll like that."

"Ever made any mocassins, Carson?" Mr Mulwin asked. "If you haven't, now's your big chance."

"Don't mind him," Lottie said, "Mr Mulwin is our resident tease."

"Bridge, moccassins," Mr Carson said in a confused tone. "I thought I came here for therapy, to find out why I don't tick."

"It takes time," Mrs Judson said in an unexpectedly motherly tone. "Some people get worse before they get better, but others start getting better right away. I can see you are one of the latter kind."

"Why thank you," Mr Carson said. "Kind words are always welcome, and no doubt a help. Once when Judy Garland tried to kill herself, I heard a newsboy running through the street shouting, 'Judy's got a sore t'roat!' It made an impression. What a thing to joke about, I thought at the time. All I really did was scratch myself a few times, and here I am in a hospital for the mentally disturbed. It almost strikes me as funny."

(169)

Mrs Brice gave him a kindly look. "You weren't really serious: I mean, as they said, you were signaling. Now you have to work out what you were signaling about. The doctors are quite a help, there."

"What about the people who really do kill themselves?" Bertha said. "You ought to give them some credit."

2

"It was nice of you to let me invite myself to tea," Maureen said. "One gets into a round of habits, and I mean to pay calls, and then I find I've put them off and put them off."

"How is everyone at your lovely home?" Mag asked. She poured Maureen's tea and passed the cup to her. "I half expected Biddy to be with you. Now there's a person who fascinates me—so active for her years, such a fund of memories."

"I thought I'd just slip out and pay a call without Biddy, dearly as I love her. It doesn't do to become too dependent on another person's company: we won't always have her with us. Everyone is fine. The twins, and Bryan. Bryan thought he was coming down with a heavy cold the other evening, but I doped him up with some antihistamines and in the morning the symptoms were all gone. Miraculous, what these modern pills can do."

"Yes," Mag said, "when they work. I ran into Mona Tromper uptown and she had a streaming cold. I told her she ought to take herself right off to bed, but with that mob of children, not to speak of their zoo, she can't afford to be sick."

"That's what Biddy attributes her good health to," Maureen said. "She says when she was bringing up the children she didn't have time to be sick, and simply lost the habit. But she's getting on, she's not so strong as she was. I have to keep an eye on her, to see she doesn't over-do. You know how she loves to bake."

"Scrumptious," Mag said. "Biddy's children. It's funny, trying to think of Bryan as a little boy. I suppose the twins somewhat resemble him as he was: a regular boy's boy."

There was a pause, then Maureen said, "Mag, there's a question I

(170)

want to ask you, though it's really none of my business."

"Oh dear, that sounds dreadfully like the sort of question that is better left unasked."

"Is there anything going on between you and Norris Taylor."

"Gossip and scandal: good heavens, is this what it means to be a widow. Maureen Delahantey, I don't know, and I don't want to know, where you've picked this story up, or if it's your own imagining, but I'm not going to discuss anythiing so vile with you. The widow and the grass-widower: oh what small minds people have."

"I know, dear, people will talk, and often with very little or no cause. But you haven't exactly answered my question."

Mag picked up her tea cup, but her hand shook so she had to set it down untasted. "Oh, I'm that cross, I can't even pick up a cup of tea. You've brought me to a pretty pass. I certainly am not going to answer your slanderous question."

"I want you to know I came here in the spirit of friendship," Maureen said. "Not to hurt you or upset you. Though if there's any truth to it, then I suppose you *should* be upset—there's Lottie Taylor and her marriage to consider."

"I'm not going to answer your question because it's just like that old chestnut, 'When did you stop beating your wife?' If I say no, you obviously will think I'm lying. You've gotten an idea planted in your mind, and I refuse to stoop to try to pluck it out. How low. Gossiped about! How would you like it if I suddenly popped out with, do you think something is going on between Bryan and Mona Tromper? How would you feel then?"

"Frankly," Maureen said, "I'd laugh in your face. I *know* Bryan Delehantey like the palm of my hand. Better, for the matter of that."

"You plainly don't know me better than any palm of your hand," Mag said. She made an effort, picked up her cup and drank from it. Then she set it down with a sharp clatter. "Nor, so far as *I* can see, do you know Norris Taylor. I don't know whether to call you a nosey-parker or a scandal-monger or both or what. That's what I have to say to you."

"To be frank with you," Maureen said, "I'm sorely tempted to put the same question to Norris Taylor himself."

(171)

"Thereby effectively destroying my friendship with both the Taylors, Lottie and Norris. You realize that, don't you? That's what will happen when this story you're spreading gets back to Lottie Taylor. Maureen, I simply wouldn't have dreamt this of you."

"My dear Mag, let me make it perfectly clear that I am *not* spreading any story. On the other hand, I'm not stone blind. I've seen you with Norris, and you have eyes for him."

"'Eyes for him.' You talk like a high school girl. I suppose you think because Bartram's gone, and I'm a widow, I have 'eyes' for anything in britches. Better keep your own eye on Bryan when I'm around—not that I expect to be seeing much of the Delahantey tribe in the near future."

"We are not a tribe," Maureen said. "And if you want to let this come between us, that's up to you. I merely came here to ask a question and give you a friendly warning and some advice—if it's necessary."

"Be honest with me, Maureen: who planted this foolish idea in your head? I would have expected you, as a friend, to stick up for me. Not come running to me with this wounding tale."

"No one plants ideas in my head. I've seen you with Norris, simpering over the card table. And Norris simpered right back, or whatever it is a man does. Even if it's no more than an idle flirtation, I thought you should know how it looks to others, and put a stop to it. For your own good reputation, and for Lottie's sake."

"Oh, bilge water. Lottie Taylor can take perfectly good care of herself. But why am I sitting here, listening to this? In my own home. You have some crust, Maureen Delahantey."

"If I'm not welcome here, then I'll leave. I'm sorry you don't know the act of a friend when you see one, Mag. My own feelings toward you haven't changed a whit: I'm simply an out-spoken, straight-forward person, there's the long and short of it."

"I'm not prepared to say," Mag said, "what my feelings are toward you. I'm too cross. Thank you very much for ruining my day." And on this note they parted.

Later in the day, or rather, quite late in the evening, over two steaming glasses of Irish coffee, Mag said to Norris, "Guess who I

(172)

saw today."

"Maureen Delahantey."

Mag started. "How in the world did you know?"

"I didn't," Norris said. "You asked me to guess, and that was my guess. I'm telepathic."

"No, honestly, did you know?"

"Honestly?"

"Yes."

"No, I didn't. I think I deserve a little praise for my acumen. And what did Mrs Delahantey, mother of men, have to say for herself? Are you girls cooking up something?"

"Me and Maureen? We've nothing to cook up: we've never been all that close. No, she simply came to tea, so big-hearted Mag did just that: gave her a cup of tea. And a small check for multiple sclerosis. At least I think that was what it was for—some one of those ailments they're always coming round about. Those dibs and dabs add up. Bartram would never have anything to do with them. But he was of a saving turn."

"Lucky for you," Norris said, "that he was. So Maureen came to tea and you gave her a contribution. Your day sounds about as exciting as mine."

Mag leaned forward and kissed him. "The day isn't over yet," she said.

"As far as excitement goes? I wonder what you're planning in that busy little head of yours."

"I'm not planning," Mag said. "I'm anticipating. Can't a girl anticipate, once in a way?"

"Who's to stop her?" Norris said. "Or how?"

At the same time, Patrick and Michael were talking in their room "Taken any more money out of mother's purse lately?" Michael asked, and snickered.

"Bung off," Patrick said.

"OK, I won't kid you," Michael said. "When is Pete going to get the grass?"

"Soon. Maybe Saturday, when he can get into the city."

"Can I buy in? I've got last week's allowance, and by Saturday I'll have this week's."

"I don't know how far an ounce will stretch," Patrick said. "Listen, you didn't say anything about this to Nick Tromper did you?"

"Maybe I did, maybe I didn't. What's the difference?"

"Plenty. We don't want the whole school knowing about it. First too many guys will want in, then somebody will squeal to their parents—'for our own good' and we'll all be in the shithouse."

"Well, Nick was there the night we turned on. He never said anything. What do you think Nick is? But I haven't told him Pete is planning to score."

"'Planning to score.' You're quite a head for someone who's only turned on once."

"Why? Have you turned on since then?"

"Yup."

"When?"

"With Pete. He only had enough for one joint, so we split it. The other afternoon."

"I bet I know what day it was," Michael said. "The one when you were so awful quiet at dinner. I wondered what was eating you."

"Pete and I went on some kind of laughing jag: every time one of us started to say something, the other one would break up laughing. It was kind of a chain reaction. So at dinner I was afraid to talk. Things were still seeming pretty funny to me."

"Where did you smoke it?"

"In Pete's backyard—you know, they've got all that shrubbery. Then we went up to his room, like we were studying. His mother was out."

"Selfish bastards."

"There wasn't enough for more than two, even if you had been around. Anyway, you're always hanging out at the Trompers'."

"No more than you're always at Pete Petrosian's. Anyway, I like Nick and his family. They're not a bit strict."

As though on cue, Bryan knocked on their door and opened it without waiting for an answer. "And when are you two planning to go to bed, I wonder?" he said. "Do you realize what time it is? Or do you want to have your allowances docked?"

(174)

"We're studying for a test tomorrow," Patrick said.

"In social studies," Michael added.

"Practicing for the school orchestra takes up a lot of our study time," Patrick said.

"And athletics," Michael added.

"If your schedule is so heavy that you can't get to sleep on time," Bryan said, "we can always cut out the athletics." But the twins knew how proud their father was of them as future letter men, and took this as the hollow threat that it was. "I suppose you've heard what happened to your friend Pete Petrosian's brother."

"You mean his brother at college," Patrick said.

"His brother who *was* at college," Bryan said.

"What happened?" Michael asked. "Did he flunk out?"

"In the biggest way," Bryan said. "He was expelled, and with a suspended sentence from the local judiciary. It seems the police staged a raid on the dormitory, and the Petrosian boy was one of those found in possession of dangerous drugs."

"His name is Timothy," Michael said.

"I don't care if his name is Holy Moses," Bryan said. "I don't want to see that younger Petrosian boy hanging around here anymore. These things run in families."

"Gee, Dad, that's not very fair. Pete . . . "

"Don't talk back to me," Bryan said.

"I'm not talking back," Patrick said. "I just wanted to say that Pete . . ."

"Do you want me to slap your face?" Bryan said. Patrick stood up without speaking. His face had turned brick red. "I've said my say about the Petrosian boys, and there isn't any more to say about it. Now both of you get to bed." Bryan left, closing the door behind him.

They had silently undressed and were in their pajamas when Maureen arrived to put in her two cents worth. "Patrick," she said, "Pete Petrosian doesn't use marijuana or LSD or any of those things, does he?"

"Of course not," Patrick said, "Where would he get them? At the A & P?"

(175)

"There's no call for sarcasm. Your father, as you may have gathered, is very disturbed by what's happened to the older Petrosian boy."

"His name is Timothy," Michael said.

"Timothy," Maureen said. "I personally don't believe in damning the one boy for his brother's fault. But you must take what your father said seriously. He means it, as you may have gathered."

"I sit next to Pete in half my classes," Patrick said. "For Christ's sake."

"Don't curse and blaspheme at your mother," Maureen said. "Apologize this minute."

"I'm sorry, Mom," Patrick said. "It's that Dad made me sore—he's so unreasonable. It's not Pete's fault if Timothy got in dutch."

"I realize that, and that's why I came up here. Your father feels a great concern, though, about drug abuse and the younger generation. I don't know what he'd do if he ever thought either of you were mixed up in something like that. I really don't."

"Don't worry, Mom," Michael said. "We're only high school kids, and there's never been any trouble at the school that I know of."

"No," Maureen said, "I know there hasn't. But an ounce of prevention is worth a pound of cure. I see it your father's way, but I see it your way too. I have faith in my two fine upstanding boys." She kissed them both and left the room.

"This is a fine how-do-you-do, or balls up," Michael said. "You realize that the cops where Tim was at college are likely to get in touch with the ones here? Suppose they raid the Petrosian's? And find Pete with a nice fresh ounce of grass stashed away?"

"I know," Patrick said. "Maybe we could hide it here."

"Don't talk crazy. You know Grandma Biddy is always going through our drawers, 'just to straighten up a little.'"

"There's the garage," Patrick said.

"And then Dad will decide to give it a good turning out, and the jig will be up. You can forget about here."

"What about Nick Tromper? Anything goes at the Tromper's—I mean, they don't check up on him all the time."

"Then you'd have to cut us both in," Michael said.

(176)

"I'll talk to Pete about it," Patrick said, "and see what he thinks."

"And I'll talk to Nick," Michael said. "Goodnight, meathead."

"Try not to fart in your sleep," Patrick said, "and gas us both to death."

3

"Mr Mulwin," Bertha said, "as long as you're posing for Mrs Taylor anyway, could I try to sculpt a head of you? I won't make it funny this time. Not on purpose, anyway."

"Be my guest, Bertha," Mr Mulwin said. "This reminds me of the time Mrs Mulwin and I went to Miami Beach. There was nothing to do but sit."

"Oh dear," Lottie said. "I hope you're not getting bored and want to quit. Yesterday I thought I was beginning to get a real likeness; but today I don't know. Every stroke seems a mistake."

"Don't worry," Mr Mulwin said, "I won't quit on you. Lord knows, I've nothing better to do with my time. I'm resigned to the fact that my business can either run itself or else go to hell in a handbasket. Imagine, at my age, starting from scratch again as a pharmacist. Working for someone else. I'm not sure I could stomach it."

"I don't suppose it will come to that," Mrs Judson said. "You probably have a loyal staff, plugging away at their appointed tasks. I know the fellows who work for Sam would do *anything* for him."

"There's much more loyalty in the business world than is commonly believed," Mrs Brice said.

"As the only business man here, I'll take that as a personal compliment," Mr Mulwin said. As though summoned, Mr Carson appeared in the doorway.

"Is this the place where I can reveal my complete lack of manual dexterity?" he asked.

"Double damnation," Lottie said. "Excuse me, Mr Carson, I was talking to myself. My own dexterity is letting me down badly today."

"How do you do? I am Miss Pride," Miss Pride said. "Let's see what we can interest you in. Moccasins, perhaps?"

"I don't really need a pair of mocassins," Mr Carson said. "I have several pairs of slippers—they get given to me at Christmas. What's that Mrs Brice and Mrs Judson are doing?"

"Making knotted belts," Miss Pride said. "Once you've mastered the simple, basic knot, you'll find yourself whizzing along. Care to give it a try? It would make a lovely present for Mrs Carson."

"It's really simplicity itself," Mrs Brice said. "I'm on my tenth. Don't know what I'm going to do with them—try and palm them off on the next church bazaar, most likely."

"I don't know," Mr Carson said querulously. "When I say I'm not dexterous, I mean it. I never have been sure which is the right knot for shoe laces."

"Still, your shoes *do* get tied," Miss Pride coaxed.

"Somehow or other," Mr Carson said. "Are moccasins very complicated?"

"No more than belts," Mrs Judson said. "I'm not handy either, but after a while you get the hang of the thing. Not that I'm a knotter in the same class as Mrs Brice."

"Don't be modest," Mrs Brice said. "You've come along beautifully."

"If I weren't nailed to this chair," Mr Mulwin said, "I'd challenge you to a hot game of gin rummy."

"That I'll take you up on, sooner or later," Mr Carson said. "My wife and I exchange thousands across the board—all in fun, of course."

"Of course," Mr Mulwin said. "I wasn't suggesting we play for money: gambling is not one of my vices."

"I see no harm," Lottie said, "in a game of bridge at a quarter a corner, or even a twentieth of a cent a point."

"One thing leads to another," Mr Mulwin said darkly.

"Are you talking about my drinking?" Lottie said sharply.

"Great Scot, no!" Mr Mulwin said.

"Oh, do you have a drinking problem, too?" Mr Carson asked. "I've belonged to AA for years. Believe me, it's a struggle, when you

(178)

get to feeling low. Not to knock back a few, I mean. I tried to cut my wrists, but I didn't take a drink. I guess I can take some pride in that. No pun intended, Miss Pride."

"We also have finger painting," Miss Pride said. "That may sound childish on the face of it, but many patients find getting in there and messing around in the paint has a physical side to it that relaxes their tensions."

"I have no tensions," Mr Carson said. "The pills they give me, I'm half-asleep on my feet."

"Mr Mulwin," Lottie said, "I'm going to release you from your vows. Portraiture is beyond me."

"Oh dear," Mrs Judson said. "And I thought it was going so nicely."

"Hey," Bertha said, "What about me? I just got started."

"Then it's not too late to stop," Mr Mulwin said, getting to his feet. "Frankly, I didn't realize how irksome posing would be. Not that there's anything else I'd rather be doing." He turned to Mr Carson. "Gin rummy?"

"Boy," Bertha said, "you're sure a big help."

"Oh, come now," Mr Mulwin said, "there's Mrs Brice and Mrs Judson, both sitting there as still as you could wish."

"Dr Kearney," Miss Pride said, "would, I think, encourage Mr Carson to try his hand at something in craft therapy. It's always good to participate, and there's the afternoon for cards."

"Orders from headquarters," Mr Carson said. "Looks like the gin rummy will have to wait."

"I'm going to scrape you right off the canvas, Mr Mulwin," Lottie said, "and try my hand at a still life. In fact, flowers." She left the room, and soon returned carrying a pot of shrubby yellow chrysanthemums. The pot was wrapped in silver foil and Lottie said, "*This* will have to come off. I haven't a clue as to how to render silver, short of using silver paint, and that's not how they do it."

"With blue, gray and white," Miss Pride said, "I think you could manage."

"No thanks," Lottie said. "I'll content myself with the plain red pot."

"As you wish," Miss Pride said in an uppity tone. "After all, it is *your* painting."

"Precisely," Lottie said, busily scraping away the last traces of Mr Mulwin.

"Mrs Brice," Bertha said, "is it OK if I do you?"

"Surely," Mrs Brice said. "It's all right if I move a little now and then, isn't it? I don't mean run around the room, just not get cramped."

"All you have to do," Bertha said, "is keep knotting and not run out on me like Mr Mulwin. I'm only aiming at a general impression."

"You can't have it all your own way, Bertha," Mr Mulwin said.

"So I've noticed," Bertha said. "Now, if you don't mind, I'm trying to concentrate."

"Why don't you sit next to me, Mr Carson?" Mrs Judson said. "I'm slower than Mrs Brice, so it will be easy for you to see how the knot is tied."

"I'll set you up," Miss Pride said, "and get you started. Here's a frame, and here are some cords from which to choose the colors you prefer. I . . ."

"I think today," Mr Carson said with unusual firmness, "I'll just watch. Then I'll know whether this is something I want to get into. I wouldn't care to get started and then lose interest."

Mrs Judson was soon demonstrating which string went over which and enjoined him, "And always pull the knot really tight, or it comes out looking funny. The first belt I made hung all crooked, because I didn't do that."

"I love the red, white and blue one you made," Lottie said to Mrs Brice. "It's what they call really snappy."

"Do you really like it?" Mrs Brice said. "Then I'll make you a present of it."

"Would you? How kind, how like you. I have a white linen it would be just the thing with."

"If there are free belts going around," Bertha said, "I could use some."

"Could you?" Mrs Brice said. "Well, I'll display my handiwork to you and you can pick one out for a memento. A few I'm reserving for myself, and this black and brown I'm making now is for Mr Brice. It will make a nice sports effect with his summer slacks."

"I wish I was dead," Mr Carson said.

"No you don't," Mrs Judson said.

"You'll get over that," Mrs Brice said, "when you've been here awhile."

"You see?" Bertha said. "Nobody around here ever believes anything you say. If the man says he wishes he was dead, he ought to know what he's talking about. Not that I believe him myself. Otherwise he would have killed himself, not just made a mess of it."

"I don't see how knotting messy belts is going to get me over the way I feel. I wish I could get over the idea that there might be an afterlife—I wouldn't care to go from bad to worse."

"You're going to die sometime," Bertha said cheerfully, "then you'll find out. Dollars gets you doughnuts there isn't any. Afterlife, I mean. But I don't know: I have a mystical streak and believe in taking it as it comes. Om. Why don't you try Zen meditation? Since you don't want to do anything else."

A nurse came in and summoned Mrs Brice away. After a while she returned with two pink spots in her cheeks. "Guess who's going to be released," she said.

"Oh Fanny," Lottie said. "I'd give you a hug only I'm all over paint. That's the most marvelous news."

"Congratulations," Mr Carson said. "I wondered what you were doing here anyway. You seem quite rational and capable to me."

"I wasn't when I came here," Mrs Brice said. "In my own way I felt about as low as you do. Oh dear, I feel all a-twitter. Do you think I'll really be able to cope? And not slide back?"

"I'm certain of it," Lottie said. "You've regained your natural equilibrium. It was temporarily shaken, but now you've got it back. We must promise to keep in touch."

"I'll be coming back for our evening sessions for a while," Mrs Brice said. "And to see Dr Kearney. An easing-off process."

Mr Mulwin, Mrs Judson and Miss Pride joined in the general congratulations.

"It hardly seems worth while going on with this belt," Mrs Brice

(181)

said. "Still, if I knot away today and tomorrow morning—I'm not leaving until tomorrow afternoon—I might get it finished." She seated herself and went on with her deft handiwork.

"It's a challenge," Bertha said, "to see how much of a likeness I can get before you leave. Onto the ramparts, men."

"What do you mean by that?" Mr Carson said.

"I'm telling myself to get a move on," Bertha said.

"I think I'll go lie on my bed," Mr Carson said.

"Oh," Miss Pride said, "that isn't encouraged during the daytime. Not without special permission, that is."

"Oh, go ahead and try it," Bertha said. "You might get in forty winks before one of the nurses chases you out."

"Bertha," Mrs Judson said, "you're being the devil's advocate."

"If your medication is making you groggy," Lottie said, "you ought to tell Dr Kearney. He may change it, or give you permission to nap—he's not altogether heartless."

"I should say not," Mrs Brice said.

Dr Kearney came into the room. "Ah," he said, "here you are Mr Carson. I wonder if we might step along to my office for a little chat?"

Mr Carson silently rose to his feet. "Busy as beavers," Dr Kearney said, smiling beneficently. "A pleasant sight."

After he and Mr Carson left, Bertha said, "And a big pooh to you. With knobs on."

"Oh dear," Mrs Judson said.

"Why Bertha," Mrs Brice said, "you imp."

"Oh dear," Mrs Judson reiterated. "I made a mistake way back here and I'll have to undo all this work. Or should I just let it pass? Who'll notice? Who'll ever wear the belt?"

"Better to go back and make it right," Mrs Brice said. "You'll never feel satisfied if you don't."

"I suppose you're right," Mrs Judson said. "Imagine, worrying feeling guilty over a teeny mistake in a stupid belt."

"It's not stupid," Lottie said. "It's going to be a very pretty belt, and finishing it will give you satisfaction. You'll see that I'm right."

"Sometimes, Mrs Taylor," Mrs Judson said stiffly, "you talk as though you were on the staff."

(182)

"I was merely speaking from my personal experience. I didn't mean to sound superior—especially after the hash I made of Mr Mulwin here."

"What's that you're saying about me?" Mr Mulwin said. "I must have dozed off there for a moment."

"I was only saying that I'd made a hash of your portrait. And I'm not sure I'm going to do any better with these chrysanthemums. Perhaps I should go back to invented and recollected subjects. They don't tie you down so."

Chapter XI

1

"A fine thing," Bryan said, "consorting with dope addicts and worse, dope peddlers. That's what the law says: over a certain amount of marijuana, and he's a resale man. Corruption, crime and corruption."

"But he's not yet sixteen," Biddy moaned. "Sure they'll take that into account. There's some older person behind this, hid it on him in his clothes when he felt the law closing in. What about that Jewish boy—never can remember his name—but I sure don't trust the look of him."

"Fatso Calabash," Patrick offered.

"That's what he's called," Michael said. "Big sissy, he'd be too scared to get mixed up in anything like *this*."

"While you two he-men wouldn't, I suppose." Bryan clattered his fork on his dessert plate, whence the pie was eaten.

"I never bought any grass or dope or anything off anybody," Patrick said vehemently.

"Me too," Michael said.

"All I have to say," Bryan said, "is that it was pretty astute of the coach to do a clothes search while you were doing your gymnastics."

"He didn't have the right," Patrick burst forth.

"Yes, he didn't have the right," Michael said firmly. "We're free white citizens."

"The color of your skin doesn't enter into it," Maureen said. "Though I admit I have my own doubts about the legality of the proceedings. You have to trust people, even when you're wrong. I think."

"Yes," Biddy said, "trusting people, it's the only way or else you find crime even where it isn't. I read somewhere that 'grass' or 'pot' is much less harmful to the system than cocktails. I think it was in the *Reader's Digest*, though it doesn't sound like them much does it?" She paused. "I wonder just what this high they talk about is like? Wouldn't know where your Gran could get a joint, would you boys?" said the saucy old lady.

The twins remained silent.

"Even on a momentous night like this," Bryan said, "I don't suppose your homework is going to do itself. You're excused."

The boys, in a flurry of thank yous and thank you ma'ams, left the table and, goosing each other on, began the ascent to their room.

"Would you listen to that," Bryan said. "Elephants at the water hole."

"They do sound rather like whales with shoes on," Maureen said.

On loud feet, Bryan marched quickly to the foot of the stairs. "You two, back down here." He was obeyed. "I want you to go up stairs quietly, like civilized men, one step at a time, and don't kick the riser. No, not you Michael. Patrick can go first. And the next one who lets the.toilet seat bang down gets the belt."

When they had achieved the seclusion of their room, and spread out books and papers, Patrick tip-toed to the door, opened it a crack, found the coast was clear of spies, and tip-toed back to his chair.

"Where'd you hide your stash?" he muttered to his twin.

"In my book bag, in my locker at school."

"Jee-zuz! Suppose they shake down the lockers? They got all the combinations to the locks!"

"I know," Michael said. "Why do you think I'm sitting here shitting brick turds? What about yours?

"My brick turds? Never use 'em."

"Your stash, your stash," Michael said.

"Smoked it up."

"Where? And when and who with?"

"Never mind. Just never mind."

"Never mind that?" Bryan demanded, entering swiftly in his stocking feet.

"Hunh?" Patrick said. "I was asking Michael a question about French and he wasn't sure of the answer so I said, 'Oh never mind." I'll figure it for myself. It's better that way, you learn more."

It was Bryan's turn to say, "Hunh." He went on, "I think that coach wasn't so dumb and we're going to have a little shake down cruise right here. Clear out your dresser drawers, one item at a time, one drawer at a time. No Michael, Patrick can go first. You study."

The search seemed to take forever, and the twins were even subjected to a pat-down search, as though by a cop in a TV show. Michael only yielded keys, some change, his good luck silver dollar bill clip (empty of bills) and an unsigned mash note which Bryan would ordinarily have gone into in depth. Bryan brightened when he found a lump in one of Patrick's pockets, but it turned out to be only a bonker on a dirty string. "Throw that away," the tyrant commanded.

Michael might as well have saved himself his worry and fret. At a special meeting of the faculty a locker search had been proposed by the coach and voted down by his peers. He was a well hated man by his fellow teachers: "Come on you book worms, how am I going to make athletes and men out of you or do you just want to be flabby book worms?" Words such as these had filtered back and created a solid block against him. The music teacher was his especial enemy, feeling that his area was in particular under attack. Even his coeval, the girls' gym teacher voted him down. But then, she was young and progressive and believed more in eurhythmics, with a soupçon of Zen, than in volley ball and other creators of ugly lumpy legs.

(187)

2

"Oh Norris Norris Norris. Yes yes like that. And like that too. And like that too. Oh Norris Norris Norris. Oh do that again. To feel your big thing in me squishing and pushing around. Oh Norris Norris Norris your tool! Your tool! Keep working at it baby. Let's try to come at the same time. Tool tool tool. Norris Norris Norris lover man. I think I'm going to shoot. Make an effort and you come too right at the same time. Oh Norris it feels so g-o-o-d!" Mag Carpenter was a chirrupy little thing, with a cunt as big as a garden hat.

3

The fire occurred in the kitchen area: some fault in the wiring of the electric coffee urn. It began to melt the vulcanite counter top. Clouds of yellowish smoke seethed into the corridor. An alert nurse sounded the alarm.

All those fire drills at school paid off. The last of the patients in the psychiatric wing (the clinic took up one floor of a wing of a large general hospital) were filing onto the lawn as the first fire truck roared up, siren sounding, bell clanging. First off was the mascot, a large spotted dog who stood to one side—well trained beast—at point toward the fire. "Like a pagan rite," someone averred.

Only Bertha gave tongue: always quick to seize any opportunity to act out her personal drama which might be entitled, "The Sufferings of Bertha." She was a deep sleeper and her sense of drama did not come alive until they were herded in orderly lines on the lawn. A light mist was falling on them and on the firemen in their impressive black slickers, Wellington boots and characteristic coal scuttle hats, dragging in the python of the thick and phallic canvas hose.

Bertha wound up to scream, like the beginning of a siren's wail. Lottie grabbed her by an upper arm, digging her fingers in hard, and shook Bertha until her teeth rattled.

"You just stop that," Lottie hissed. "You stop spreading fear and alarm. Panic! A lot of these patients are sicker than you are, and they're acting sensible." Shake, shake, rattle, rattle. "You stand up straight and keep your mouth shut or I'm going to slap your face until your ears ring." There was that in Lottie's tone that caused the usually irrepressible Bertha to straighten up and fly right.

The sight was a most impressive one: mist falling on the silent files of patients, in different degrees of negligee, the trained nurses shuttling swiftly among them, doing a kind of bed check and disclosing wonderful memories, so sure of who was in their charge, the firemen moving purposely through lanes in the crowd that cleared as at the waving of a magic wand. Out of the side door and kitchen windows still poured the acrid smoke and a hissing of steam.

"If only Mrs Brice were still here!" Lottie softly cried out. "How she would enjoy it. So quiet and reticent yet always ready for a little excitement. A deep one, yes, and deep one. Kind and good." She addressed a young man on her not-Bertha side. He was a new patient and had not been known to speak. In fact his only notable act to date was pouring his oatmeal and milk on the floor, which he docilely cleaned up at the behest of a nurse.

Lottie and the night's excitement stirred him to speak. "Of glog," he seemed to say.

"Dear oh dear," Lottie said to him, "I hope this won't interfere with my dismissal tomorrow. The Lord knows, I've earned it."

Bertha seized the diversion of Lottie's attention to stick her tongue out at her. She stuck it out good and far.

A fireman, overcome by smoke, was carried out on a stretcher. "Won't be going back in there right away," a fireman remarked to a passing nurse.

"I should hope not," the nurse replied. "Why, even out here the smell gives me vertigo. What *is* that burning?"

"Smouldering vulcanite," replied the fireman, and went about his business.

Finally, the damp and shivering patients were allowed to return to their murky quarters, where a horrible smell hung in the air. At the door, the head night nurse stood with a clipboard, checking off each patient as he or she passed in. There were puddles on the hall floor and the kitchen was a sight.

"No goggling about," the head nurse said, "get to bed and try to sleep. Or at least rest. Rest is sometimes as refreshing as sleep," she improbably added.

"The night of the fire!" Lottie caroled. "The night of the fire! Who will ever forget?"

In the seeming safety of her room, Bertha cut loose. "I can't breathe! I can't breathe this killing smog! It smells like death! Oh Christ, oh shit, I'm suffocating, asphyxiation, horrible death and I'm so young and practically a virgin!" She pressed her face to the coarse mesh of the window screen and inhaled loud gulps and gasps of air.

A nurse entered on heavy military feet, carrying a wet washcloth. She grabbed Bertha, wheeled her around and with the wash cloth smartly slapped her cheeks. "Hysterics—that's all we need, you spoiled brat." She shook Bertha, whose head snapped back and forth while her messy hair flaired and bushed out. "Get in that bed and shut up or I'll give you something you'll never forget, trouble-making bitch." She released Bertha, who with a surprising show of dignity turned and got into bed and faced the wall.

Chapter XII

1

It was afternoon in a dusty, stale-beer smelling hard-hat bar. A few morose topers leaned on the bar and Mag and Norris sat in a booth at the back, the table ornamented with a drink slopped checked cloth and salt crystals off pretzels. As a hideaway, they could not have chosen a spot where they could be more conspicuous; still, it was unlikely any of their set would wander into this seedy setting.

Mag was acting kittenish, but her hands in her lap flexed their talons, like a cat in a lap kneading bread ("Ouch, pussy!"). There was a distinct air of the dentate vagina. Norris looked sourly at his too-sweet scotch sour. "Always order straight booze in a joint like this. Bourbon and a beer chaser: a boiler maker, they're called."

"I heard of an amusing little drink the other bridge game," Mag said lightly. "A rusty nail, it's called: scotch with a dash of Drambuie. Of course the scotch must be of the best," she added, and gave a little shudder as she looked at the unlikely rot gut lined up behind the bar. "So Mary Lottie's coming home. How nice."

"Yes," Norris said, "it is. I wasn't cut out to be a bachelor."

"Norris," Mag said in a gentle, hurt tone, "aren't you forgetting something?"

Norris looked puzzled. "What?"

"Us."

"Are we going to review all that again? I thought I made it clear: I'm a married man: a happily married man."

"And where does that leave me?"—in plaintive tones.

"Just where I found you, my merry widow." Norris gave what for him could only be called an evil chuckle. "To be blunt, we have now had our last roll in the hay."

"Oh. How coarse. I love you. I *can't* let you go like this. I won't do it. You've committed me to you."

"How are you folks doing?" asked the barkeep. "Get you anything?"

"No, thank you," Mag said.

"Yes," Norris said. "Two more of the same and could you make them less sweet?"

"Can do; will do." Something about the way Norris and Mag were dressed gave the owner hopes of a rise in the world.

"I think," Mag said, "I will have to have a little talk with Lottie. A chat, explaining to her just how things stand."

"They don't stand. Whatever we had between us—and I admit I enjoyed it—is over. Finis. Quits."

"Oh?" Mag said. "I wonder."

"Don't bother your thick skull with wondering. Even if Lottie dropped dead today I'd never go to bed with you again. Can you grasp that idea?"

"Oh yes. But I still think a little talk is in order. To clear the air."

"I admit the air in here is not very clear. But I can tell you one thing: if you ruin my marriage I'll kill you. I have a gun and I'll use it. I'm a one woman man and that woman is my wife."

Mag picked at the table cloth. "Norris, I love you in this primitive mood. It gives me little chills. Couldn't you take the afternoon off and come home with me?"

"No. N-o. Christ, you are dumb."

(192)

"Well, thanks a lot. Thanks for nothing. I'm not going to forget this right away!"

"Good. Now you're catching on."

2

When the earth was thrown into Biddy's grave and rattled on the coffin, and the priest pronounced the fatal, final words, Bryan broke into terrible dry sobs and threw his arms around his wife. "Honey, honey, you're all I have left. Let me die first. Don't you desert me."

"There there there," Maureen said softly. "There there. She had a wonderful life, happy and good right to the very end."

Michael was crying unashamedly. Patrick stood numbly still. All the parish was there to honor the matriarch. In the background Mag and Lottie stood side by side and dabbed at their eyes. Norris stood with clenched hands and stared at the sod.

That night the Delahanteys retired in silence, forgetting to let Twing in. Maureen lay wide-eyed, mourning. After she thought Bryan asleep, he suddenly rolled over, grabbed her night dress and ripped it up the front. He began to bite her nipples as he forced his hard cock into her. His tears fell on her breasts. This was not like them. Bryan was naturally a rough man, but Maureen had tamed him to be gentle. Tonight she slid her hands under his pajama jacket and dug her nails into his flesh. "Fuck me," she said, "fuck me hard make me feel it." She had never used the word "fuck" before in her life.

In the twins' room, a whispered drama went on.

"For the love of Pete," Patrick said, "quit jerking off. You're even shaking *my* bed."

"Oh shut up," Michael said. "I can't sleep if I don't get my nuts off."

"You're going to shake the whole house. Dad will be in here with a strap. You'll get it and then he'll blame me too."

"Framistan to you. If you can't sleep go let the cat in. She's been yowling for an hour."

(193)

"You do it."

Michael chuckled. "I can't. I'm otherwise occupied. Sweet shit, I'm going to come. Oh hot damn what a load."

"You disgust me."

"Go soak your head. I'm going to sleep."

3

A new liberalism reigned at the Norris Taylor residence. Fat old Deirdre lay lumped in a Victorian chair. Her head was lain against one over-stuffed arm, dribble running out of the corners of her mouth. A picture of contentment.

The Delahanteys, sans twins, had come to dinner and a rubber of bridge.

"Did you notice what Maureen was wearing?" Lottie asked Norris, who was catching up on the evening paper which the party had postponed.

"Hmmm?" he said.

"Maureen's dress. It could only be called definitely sexy. Frankly, I was afraid a tit was going to leap out of her corsage and shoot me in the eye."

"You wouldn't look so bad in one of those outfits yourself."

"Franks a lot. You know you'd hate it. My husband, Norris Taylor, may vote Democrat but at heart he's a very conservative man. I think what it is is Biddy's passing on. It's had a liberating effect. Don't misunderstand me: they loved Biddy—we all did—but, still, there's a second honeymoon in the air."

"They're not the only ones on a second honeymoon." Norris put down his paper and obscenely rubbed his crotch.

"Why Norris Morton Taylor, you old reprobate." Lottie sighed. "I have to admit it. A shot of vodka would taste mighty good to yours truly."

"You'll get sick: remember you're full of Antabuse."

"Have no fears. Mary Charlotte Norton Taylor has bent her last bender. God willing. You know what was funny? I *enjoyed* mixing

(194)

and serving the cocktails. Didn't feel a shadow of a desire to have one myself. I only felt sad at dinner, when I couldn't join in the toast to Biddy's memory. No-Cal cherry. Ugh. And now shall we talk about Mag?"

"I feel no need to," Norris said. Deirdre sighed loudly and had a fine hair-scattering scratch, then switched her dribbling head to the other arm and proceeded to saturate that.

"Oh, Norris, hubby, let's just take it out for a trot in the air. All I really want to know is this: it is over, isn't it?"

Norris leapt to his feet. "Yes," he roared, "totally over. You can't imagine what a numbskull that woman is. Honestly I only thought I felt a physical need, but I was really punishing myself. The prattle I had to put up with!"

Lottie laughed, heartily. "Yes the little dear does run on so. And the mileage she gets out of her widowhood! You'd think nobody's husband had ever passed the bourne before."

"You can say that again."

"No, thanks. Once was enough. You know we, we really must put our heads together and dig up a Mr Right for her. She has scorpions in her pants. I don't want her to start making passes at the grocery boy." She laughed. "Who is about seventy five and very dark complected."

"Tell me the truth," Norris said. "How did you find out? I was really very discreet."

Lottie gave a horse laugh. "Come here," she said. Norris went and knelt by her chair and put his head in her middle aged womanly lap. "Why, even the girl at the checkout knew about it."

"I don't believe you."

"As a matter of fact, no one told me: though I could tell Maureen had something she *wanted* to tell me, which rather aroused my suspicions. No, truthfully, it was at Biddy's funeral service. Mag thought I wasn't observing because of my hankie but she gave you one long Medea look and the truth was out. I am not deaf, dumb and blind and I am observant. Ouch. Norris Taylor, you're biting me."

"I am?" Norris said in innocent tones.

"We'd better get these things off. I don't want my new pongee

(195)

ruined. Come Deirdre. The dishes can definitely keep. But we are going to help Mag. You owe her that much. How about the coach? He's single isn't he?"

"And in my opinion as queer as a three dollar bill. He just wants to worship the young athletic form divine. Screw the coach. To hell with Mag. Let's get in bed."

4

As a matter of fact, Mag Carpenter was in hell.

She took the elevator to the floor Norris's firm was on. She looked pert in her tricorn hat sprinkled with pansies.

Mag walked down the hall and stood outside Norris's door. The door opened and a secretary came out. "Can I help you?" she asked.

"No, no," Mag said. "I'm just waiting for someone." The secretary vanished into the elevator (self operated) Mag had come up in.

It was a long corridor, with a terrazzo floor. Many silent doors with panes of pebble glass let into them opened onto it. At either end was a large plate glass window. Mag strolled to one of these and stood staring out.

She opened the window and out she went.

The trim had recently been painted and from the hand grips dripped stalactites of dried cream colored paint. Mag felt to see if the window was latched shut. It was not. She tugged at the grips. The new paint job had sealed it shut.

"Damn," she muttered.

Mag thought of taking off a shoe and battering the glass, but it looked thick. The battering would just call attention to her and make her look silly. She put the shoe back on and looked down. There in the parking lot was her sky blue convertible. She sighed and swore again.

Mag turned and retraced her steps. As she passed Norris's office she stuck her tongue out and made a vulgar noise. The elevator came, bearing the same secretary. She gave Mag a curious look. Mag stuck her tongue out at her too. The secretary gasped and hurried on her appointed round. Mag descended.

Mag was soon seated at the wheel of her car, out of the parking lot and headed for her meticulous home.

Printed August 1978 in Santa Barbara & Ann Arbor
for the Black Sparrow Press by Mackintosh and Young
& Edwards Brothers Inc. Cover drawing by
Jane Freilicher. Design by Barbara Martin.
This edition is published in paper wrappers;
there are 500 hardcover trade copies; & 226 copies have been
handbound in boards by Earle Gray &
are numbered & signed by the author.

Photo: Ruth Kligman

James Schuyler, poet, novelist and critic, is the au-
thor of "The Picnic Cantata," a text for music by
Paul Bowles, and two previous novels, *Alfred and
Guinevere* and *A Nest of Ninnies* (written in conjunc-
tion with John Ashbery). His collections of poetry
include *Freeley Espousing, The Crystal Lithium* and
Hymn to Life. He was formerly on the staff of The
Museum of Modern Art and an associate editor of
Art News, and he continues to write occasional pieces
on art. He makes his home in New York.